THE CONDUIT AND OTHER VISIONARY TALES OF MORPHING WHIMSY

by
Richard Gessner

Rain Mountain Press
New York City

THE CONDUIT AND OTHER VISIONARY TALES OF MORPHING WHIMSY

ISBN: 978-0-9981872-1-1

Rain Mountain Press
www.rainmountainpress.com

Cover art: "Orphan Floss Circus" by Richard Gessner

Layout and cover design:
David G. Barnett
Fat Cat Graphic Design
fatcatgraphicdesign.com

The Author dedicates this work to
Joan Sonnenfeld,
Brian McCormack,
Vincent Czyz,
and to the memory of his parents,
Patricia Vanat
and A.W. Gessner.

ACKNOWLEDGMENTS

Grateful acknowledgment is made to the following magazines in which some of this work was first published.

AIR FISH an anthology of speculative works: “The Zoobrary” “The Olfactory Inversion” COE REVIEW, FICTION INTERNATIONAL, The Fool issue: “Excerpts from the diary of a Neanderthal Dilettante” SEIN UND WERDEN, The Unnatural World issue, & SKIDROW PENTHOUSE 18: “The Conduit” “Arbitration, At Goo...” RAMPIKE, The Subterfuge issue: “The Ink Device” HAPPY 11 & FLESH & BLOOD #8 Tales of Dark Fantasy & Horror: “The Sleepwalker” SKIDROW PENTHOUSE 19: “The Unicyclist” HAPPY 5, FURIOUS FICTIONS, MALLIFE: “Status” OINK! 19, SEIN UND WERDEN Wunderkammer issue “The Embezzler” THE PANNUS INDEX, SURREALIST PARADIGM: “The Parallel Between the Cake and the Tail” ICE RIVER 5: “The Funeral Service” ANOTHER CHICAGO MAGAZINE 23, 580 SPLIT issue 2: “The Hermit” (short versions) RAMPIKE, the propaganda issue, THE ACT, SEIN UND WERDEN, metropolis issue, SUB ROSA 24 “The Ball” (various versions) RAMPIKE, the food issue: “The Man in the Couch” ANOTHER CHICAGO MAGAZINE 18 “The Battery Song” THE FICTION REVIEW #4 “Caviar” AILERON: “The Unpatented Universe” AIEEE: “Vanity” LOST & FOUND TIMES 21/22: “White Fuzz”

Table of Contents

Introduction to Richard Gessner's The Conduit and Other Visionary Tales of Morphing Whimsy

by Vincent Czyz

The Montclair Book Center has been on Glenridge Avenue in Montclair, NJ, for decades; how many exactly I don't know, but I've been foraging among its shelves since the late '80s. For a number of years the shop supported Page One, an on-premises café, which became the haunt of local artists, writers, and savants. In 1997 I was in Page One when I saw, on the community bulletin board, a posting for a writers' group recruiting new members. I'd always worked alone, but I liked the idea of a loosely organized collective and found a seat—a metal folding chair—at the next meeting.

The group consisted of eight or nine writers working in poetry and prose, from the fantasy novel to the personal essay. Generally we took pages home with us, but at the second or third meeting I attended, several members read their work aloud. One of the authors was a tall man with thick glasses and a stentorian voice. He read a story about a sleepwalker skating on a single rusty skate across frozen rain puddles, his eyes "blind to an inky tutu fungus of old newspapers encircling his waist, flaking into yellow dust with each thrust and turn." If I found the subject matter a bit unusual, I also found the language striking. I forgot the name of the story, and I forgot the names of most of the group members, which held together for about a year, but in the twenty or so years since I listened to Richard Gessner read from "The Sleepwalker," I never forgot that newspaper tutu.

I was to discover that Gessner's head is a sort of cavern piled high with such wonders—original images, fresh metaphors, mind-stretching scenarios, and alternate world orders. A sampling of the narrative set-ups in *The Conduit and Other Visionary Tales of Morphing Whimsy* hints at what the reader is in for: A war criminal takes refuge in the hollow of a tree and accretes a helmet of bird droppings; the authors of books housed in a multi-storied library are imprisoned in its basement and cross-bred to produce hybrid literary forms; platypus eggs multiply in the scrotum of a unicyclist:

> *Shining through the scrotal sac, twinkling in stars far and near,*
> *swarms of bluish eggs bulge over the saddle of the nomad's unicycle,*
> *making pedaling most difficult.*

The surreal aspects of Gessner's stories recall the work of French author Raymond Roussel (1877-1933). In Roussel's novel *Locus Solus*, for example, we encounter a scientist who has invented a balloon-powered, road-building machine, which, using human teeth of varying hues of brown, is assembling a mosaic of a Native American warrior. While this is the sort of oddity a reader shouldn't be surprised to turn up in a Gessner fiction, the language Roussel uses is Victorian in its formality and almost scrupulously objective—at least in translation—as might befit a scientist. Roussel's novel is carried not so much by his style as by an array of ingenious curiosities. Gessner strikes a more equal balance between the poetry of the prose and the parade of strangeness, between whimsical wordplay and the progression of the tale itself.

He is also relentlessly funny. Virtually every paragraph in "Excerpts from the Diary of a Neanderthal Dilettante"—the title is self-explanatory—presents the reader with material worthy of a stand-up routine:

> *Just recently we have been learning to draw Picasso running toward us holding a small pad of paper; who or what Picasso is remains to be seen. According to the professor, he doesn't exist yet. [...] Since I, the professor and my fellow students will all be fragments preserved in glass cases in natural history museums by the time Picasso is born, we have no way of knowing whether or not he was somehow involved in the arts. Perhaps I should be more skeptical, for all I know Picasso might be a ne'er-do-well who lives at the Y.M.C.A who is in a constant state of trepidation over the fact that he might be an immense ruffled pair of anthropomorphic bloomers in a world inhabited by omnipotent seamstresses who are vehemently against ruffles.*

"The Zoo-brary," mentioned above, will also produce, if not belly laughs, certainly a few inner chuckles.

> *Writers of different type, ability and degree of stature are paired up in opposite cells with facing bars so they can view only each other. Parking-ticket scribblers face classical versifiers—Subpoena makers face street poets to produce spontaneous legal writs—Seminal 'inventives' face shopworn 'derivatives' to make an accessible would-be radical with a pioneering gloss. [...]Scholarly treatise writers face gossip columnists to make high-pulp crops of academic sensation—A zoo-breeder wanders through the maze of*

hallways listening to the congress of burgeoning tete-a-tetes caught up in an infectious meld of snowballing ideas.

What Gessner does best, perhaps, is create microcosms—self-contained worlds in which he has made up the rules and established the action. I'm reminded of a drop of water, which, under van Leeuwenhoek's microscope, turned out to be teeming with alien creatures possessed of varied modes of swimming. I am reminded of Blake: Gessner dramatizes the Romantic poet's belief that there is a world in a grain of sand. "The Conduit," one of the more visionary pieces, demonstrates Gessner's ability to expand space and uncover its inhabitants in a seemingly infinite regression. It begins as the tale of a man who has been stabbed in the heart crawls into a sewer pipe to die, but the pipe is an existential anomaly—"Huge, wide, longer than all-seeing memory"—and harbors not only the wounded man, but also a good chunk of the universe. "The ancestors of the victim and assailant line up in rows facing each other, linking pinkies in a twilight square dance." The spiraling dancers create a kind of vortex, drawing in, among other things, a "millennial scorpion," transpersonal memories, reborn kamikaze pilots, opportunistic remoras, whole countries, a chorus of birds, "an old mossback snapping turtle of an unknown forbear." This is not, however, a chaotic collection of imagery summoned up to no visible purpose, but a transcendence of the familiar relationship between subject and object, the seer and the seen, victim and assailant, told in hallucinatory prose. In the end the story invites both reconciliation and redemption.

Many readers shy away from the avant-garde, finding it inaccessible, confusing, absurd, arbitrary to the point of meaningless. I myself have these issues with Andre Breton's prose experiments, Antonin Artaud's surrealist poetry,

John Ashbery's later work, many of the stories in Yoko Tawada's *Where Europe Begins*, and a dozen other contemporary books that defeated my attempts to engage with them. Gessner's writing is not of that ilk. While his literary creations don't always obey the laws of classical physics, they have an affinity for the quirks of quantum mechanics, and though they dispense with the logic of Aristotle, they replace it with the logic of dreams. Moving sometimes in a straight line, sometimes in an arabesque, the stories progress nonetheless, and the writing stirs beauty at unlit depths—like echolocations that sound out shapes in the psyche we didn't know were there. Endlessly inventive, Gessner is not interested in the arbitrary thrill; rather, he is out to inspire us to rethink our assumptions, to reframe our perspectives, to renew our ways of seeing. His writing is a funhouse mirror, distorting the empirical world in ways that, paradoxically, help us see it better.

THE ZOO-BRARY

Beneath a multi-leveled library is a basement zoo where the writers of the books above are kept.

The zoo has a honeycomb structure sectioned off by narrow hallways running between circular rows of cells filled with a diverse collection of writers.

The zoo has an optimum cross-breeding design. Writers of different type, ability and degree of stature are paired up in opposite cells with facing bars so they can view only each other.

Parking-ticket scribblers face classical versifiers—

Subpoena makers face street poets to produce spontaneous legal writs—

Seminal "inventives" face shopworn "derivatives" to make an accessible would be radical with a pioneering gloss—

The forgotten face the immortal—

The touted face the neglected—

The baroque long-winded face terse aphorists—

Scholarly treatise writers face gossip columnists to make high pulp crops of academic sensation—

A zoo-breeder wanders through the maze of hallways listening to the congress of burgeoning tete-a-tetes caught up in an infectious meld of snowballing ideas.

The drone of voices reverberates, causing the caked stratum of upper floor tome dust to shift ever so slightly. Snatches of conversation overheard by diagonally opposite cell occupants are stolen by a web of intersecting plagiarism spreading throughout the honeycomb.

Jewel-kernels lost in the generic stew of blended voices are fished out by the zoo-breeder and developed in the throes of invention while the idle plot to break through the ceilings of their cells, invading the upper floors to rewrite the books of their neighbors.

At the center of the honeycomb is an incubator where the pairs of the most promising writers chosen by the zoo-breeder are placed to mate and give birth.

When the babies are born the parents are returned to their cells. The zoo-breeder raises the children like a pedantic wet nurse, bringing them to the upper floors for the daily rigors of learning and tome dust castle building, returning them to the incubator where they work themselves up into the prime white heat of prodigyhood—producing seminal works for all posterity to feed off of.

The slow runts who fail to make their mark early, are culled from the revolutionary litter and doomed to wither in a feral state beyond the Zoo-brary walls.

When the fresh crop of genius comes of age, they are placed in their own cells opposite those of a different type, ability and stature.

The writers are rotated in their cells each time a new generation is added so new pairs face each other.

The inept and barren are weeded out to make room for the new. The promise of future progeny born of fresh pairings keeps evolution inching forward . . .

As the zoo-breeder puts the works of the new generation on the upper floor shelves, he looks out a window watching the culled orphan from a gossip columnist/classical scholar mismatch who roams the Zoo-brary grounds waiting to be let in.

Excerpts From The Diary of A Neanderthal Dilettante

January 7, Middle Paleolithic Era

We completed the tiny papier-mâché mastodons today and are about to display them on our prominent eyebrow ridges; many of us fear we will be ridiculed, because inexplicably the obtuse beasts will grasp our satirical intentions...

January 9, Paleolithic Era

Today our "history of groupies" teacher gave a lecture on the inevitability of geniuses throughout the ages building a spaceship from the countless autographs which have been requested of them; I must confess that I don't quite grasp the concept of remarkable beings in a flimsy paper construction exploring the vast frontiers of groupies, lackeys, and dabblers in other solar systems; but I don't let on to anyone about this because if I did I would undoubtedly be considered less than chic and maybe get placed in the same category as those from a regressed backwater who are still diagramming cave drawings.

January 23, Paleolithic Era

Just recently we have been learning to draw Picasso running towards us holding a small pad of paper; who or what Picasso is remains to be seen; according to the professor he doesn't exist yet. This evening I decorated several caves with thousands of images of this unknown figure and find it hard to suppress extreme satisfaction in doing so; I just hope that my feelings of mirth are not unjustified because, as the professor said, who or what Picasso is still remains to be seen. Since I, the professor and my fellow students will all be fragments preserved in glass cases in natural history museums by the time Picasso is born, we have no way of knowing whether or not he was somehow involved in the arts. Perhaps I should be more skeptical, for all I know Picasso might be a ne'er-do-well who lives at the Y.M.C.A who is in a constant state of trepidation over the fact that he might be an immense ruffled pair of anthropomorphic bloomers in a world inhabited by omnipotent seamstresses who are vehemently against ruffles.

February 5, Paleolithic Era

Today some students had a dispute over whose vertebrae in whose spine would make a better set of dominoes, those of the Neanderthal, or those of modern man; soon this frivolous activity gave way to a rally protesting against the spine becoming erect through evolutionary time. The viable alternative presented was to reverse the process of evolution so that the spine will regress into curvature so extreme it could be easily mistaken for a hula hoop; I still don't understand why such grave issues must have such frivolous conclusions.

February 20, Paleolithic Era

Today, in our "modes of appropriating the new" class the teacher presented a manuscript to the students which was written by a contemporary of those who will one day display our bones in natural history museum show cases (I am taking a special course in using the past tense in reference to events that have not happened yet) The teacher was unsure whether or not the manuscript was a criticism of some long forgotten work, or simply something indistinguishable from a patchwork quilt someone's aunt wove from grocery lists collected throughout the ages.

Predictably the class assignment is to analyze the intentions of this work (I have already completed my terse essay filled with more insights than anything manufactured in state of the art nurseries of precocity). I will thoroughly describe my adroit observations, but first here is the manuscript presented to the class: To understand Conan's collection of poems "Flowers," we must first examine several of the author's earlier works: "Circumvention and the maternal instincts toward a hot water bottle filled with ink drained from love letters drenched soaking wet in a hurricane."

This work is essentially a melodrama focusing on the concept of Machiavelli and a folk singer synthesizing their ideas in a whirlpool bath; these two characters are never mentioned in the work however. Instead the central theme deals with the hot water bottle and the various stages of the ink congealing inside it; Conan tests the ink for amorous content with litmus paper; the tragedy of this work became increasingly apparent when a vegetable strainer gets stuck inside the hot water bottle for eternity; it is subtly implied that Conan was attempting to strain all the love unrequited from the ink to appropriate it for his own martyrdom.

Halfway through this work a pervasive callousness begins when Conan installs the iron hard hot water bottle as a clapper inside a giant rubber bell used in a vast truck tire factory; it is at this point that we become aware of the truck tire molds patterned after the convolutions of museum guard brains; there is little explanation of this enigmatic subject, only Conan's envious lamenting over a fleeting white walled genius who makes long hauls across interstate highways winning fourteen Pulitzer prizes in every truckstop along the way.

The conclusion of this work seems to be a vague compensation; there are the beginnings of an epic poem based on the tragic theme of ink congealing inside a hot water bottle, but soon enough Conan goes off on a cynical tangent about how such a consolidated mass of human frailness and vulnerability could become something resembling a huge hockey puck wearing an opaque slipcover. In Conan's second work he sees himself as a pair of metaphorical swim trunks, a premise which supports his fears that his students will outgrow him; this work deals primarily a homage paid to a student who has Conan's seams altered by a tailor so he will still fit inside his teacher. This process continues until the trunks are so large that someone installs tightropes inside the legs; soon meter maids pirouette up and down the ropes juggling barren oysters; Conan is particularly bitter about this because he has unwittingly invented a metaphor for impotence. The conclusion, however, is filled with optimism (a thousand-page treatise about a flattering remark once made comparing him to a terry cloth astrodome).

February 26, Paleolithic Era

During the next five years Conan took his sabbatical and went to Africa; it was there he wrote *Scavengers Femme Fatale*, a tragedy in which he is the protagonist. Here we have a stark scene on the plains of Africa, with Conan building geysers which shoot Miss Clairol hair dye high into the sky in an attempt to dye a flock of circling vultures the same shade of blonde as actress Doris Day. A general sense of disappointment bordering on scandal begins when Conan learns that he has dyed an enclave of vultures all of whom are named Doris Day. If the Doris Day vultures are already blond; why must he attempt to dye them blond a second time?

February 29, Paleolithic Era

Conan's next work "The Pachyderm in my hairdryer" deals with the development of a curler for the trunk of a baby elephant which has become stiff from the psychological conditioning of listening to too many popular love songs based on the theme of lockjaw. He boasts of his scientific genius when he encases a chain of supermarkets inside a giant test tube made from shower curtains with daisies printed on them; he then isolates the rare strain of curler from millions of shopping housewives (apparently the daisies on the shower curtains helped him focus his critical powers to develop an orthopedic curler culture.

March 2, Paleolithic Era

Conan's next project concerns a pugilist and a theory about his cufflinks and the fillings in his teeth. According to Conan there is a gravitational force pulling the cufflinks and tooth fillings together. Predictably a tragedy takes place when the cufflinks and fillings merge at his chest, forming an unsightly metallic jewel detracting from the appearance of his virile synthetic patch of chest hair. Soon he develops a strain of tadpole which remains in the legless stage and resembles his favorite boxers; in artificial environments (aftershave ponds) he invents lily pads which resemble boxing gloves; much to his despair his creations adhere to his tragic theory; they possess replicas of his patch of synthetic chest hair which is overshadowed by the unsightly metallic jewel. Conan is furious, losing control when the metallic jewel detaches itself from the chest hair floating to the surface of the pond to sun itself on the boxing glove lily pads.

March 10, Paleolithic Era

Finally we arrive at Conan's book "Flowers" (before reviewing it I feel it necessary to discuss the illustrations because of the effect they had on one of our greatest painters; upon viewing them Chaim Soutine gave up painting meat carcasses and took up residence inside a mailbox where he composed elaborate paper dolls resembling a goat named Emily who only produces milk on leap year while spinning on a merry-go-round chandelier at the ceiling of the Waldorf Astoria hotel).

Reviewing this book I must confess that I haven't read it, and suggest that you don't read it either. I have developed a more successful means of interpreting its meaning. If you will note carefully, the poems are written in long narrow columns shaped like spinal vertebrae. If we take the book apart placing each column on top of the other we will eventually form the author's spine; perhaps this is an oblique hint that the real brilliant epic on unparalleled artistic merit is in the shoulder blades or up the back of the cranium; let us hope that the opening in his infant skull cap finally sealed up completely or else his genius and muse might fall through the opening plummeting down to the balls of the feet where it will remain unexhumed by even the most clairvoyant of orthopedic podiatrists with missiles to send the psychic contents back up to the mind.

March 19, Paleolithic Era

A pervasive callousness begins when Conan installs an iron hard hot water bottle as a clapper inside a giant rubber bell in a vast truck tire factory; at this point we become aware of truck tire molds patterned after the convolutions on museum guards' brains. Conan obviously means his students' brain convolutions. Although it is flattering to know that the imprints of one's mind will be left to posterity by way of a practical manufacturing device, I am not so naïve as not to recognize that the imprints of the brain are no more immortal than a vast corpus of measured contours of feet that have been under medical attention placed end to end forming a connected chain around the circumference of the earth, resembling Saturnian rings; somehow it is apparent that this spectacle would not become a legend in the podiatrists' hall of fame. Some fraternity brothers and I have seen fit to compose a maze from the truck tire molds and subject Conan to a rigorous obstacle course based on our collective intelligence.

March 21, Paleolithic Era

Conan's metaphorical swim trunk theme is deceptive. It isn't swim trunks our teacher is speaking of but monogrammed boxer shorts, several pairs of them which the students never outgrow. Instead a meter maid and an oyster catcher pilfer the monograms from the boxer shorts inexplicably presenting them to the public as their own invention which produces pearls while causing one to get several parking tickets (for every pearl produced one must get fourteen parking tickets) This invention becomes extremely popular because it illustrates the point that one cannot have ethereal gems without everyday petty annoyances (I truly believe that an oyster which produces parking tickets instead of pearls would be the authentic ethereal gem).

March 22, Paleolithic Era

Conan's work "Scavengers Femme Fatale" is simply a bit of veiled sarcasm; what is obvious is that the person who is attempting to dye flocks of circling vultures a Doris Day blonde with Miss Clairol hair dye geysers is really Conan trying to conceal his desire to tattoo low-brow pool hall types with the most brilliant of his students' manuscripts; I really don't see how this could work because what tattooist would have enough erudite literacy to cover each pool player with an entire student manuscript without first tattooing anchors, flags, dagger-pierced hearts and other classic retro tattoo themes in place of metaphysical observations and abstruse points which can only be grasped by an elite select few?

March 23, Paleolithic Era

The "Pachyderm in my hair dryer" is an insult Conan is directing towards his students; any association of a pachyderm with curlers is a cue for a satire about our fraternities' annual mastodon hunt. It is implied that our hunting instincts are channeled toward the practice of beauty parlor techniques; this would mean applying curlers to the mastodon as the kill is ensuing; the term "curler industry" would exist to produce enough curlers to curl the entire coat of a mastodon.

There are also oblique references to us producing cave drawings of hair dryers and beauty appliances; also hieroglyphics of the chit-chat between housewives having their hair done at the beauty parlor.

April 1, Paleolithic Era

Conan's theory about a pugilist, his cufflinks and tooth fillings is a weak attempt at satirizing evolution. The main point, however, is that he didn't think anyone enrolled in his classes was sophisticated enough to recognize that tooth fillings and cufflinks merging at the center of a patch of chest hair is the sign of modern invention triumphing over the primitive. What our teacher fails to recognize is that if we students are so primitive, then how come we control the import and export of synthetic chest hair from one epoch to another? He is oblivious to the fact that this product will be more in demand because as man evolves he will have less and less hair. Conan's concept of a tadpole remaining in the legless stage represents evolution coming to a standstill (unless it is abstaining from growing legs in order to avoid any situations where it might have to wear rollerskates; if this is the case the tadpole is so advanced in evolution it knows that the rollerskating arena outside our dormitory has been closed down) the boxing glove lily pads could only mean that Jack Dempsey originated in Claude Monet's water lily paintings...Conan's book of poems are written in long narrow columns shaped like spinal vertebrae, and when the students take the book apart placing each column on top of the other they built modern man's spine. If one were to try to build the Neanderthal's spine in such a manner it would topple over in the building process, the real brilliant epic of unparalleled artistic merit lying nearby in the shoulder blades is out of reach unless one's spine is erect.

April 9, Paleolithic Era

I questioned our teacher about the origins of vinyl. If it will not exist for another 40,000 years, then what is that thick clear plastic brace he wears to flatten his prominent eyebrow ridges actually made of?

April 17, Paleolithic Era

In our class "history of bric-a-brac and ephemeral decoration versus the disappearance of the immortal" we are learning to draw Picasso in motel room landscapes running away from us. In the beginning of the class we learned to draw the unknown, yet to be born figure running towards us holding an autograph pad, why this sudden reverse in circumstances?

August 3, Late Paleolithic Era

I am reworking my papier-mâché mastodons and plan to choreograph them against a background of pink cupcake icing (a brilliant juxtaposition designed to show how the archaic is martyred by modern day confections). I am disappointed by the crew who have reconstructed their autograph spaceship; they no longer pay close attention to me as they did in the past; to rekindle their interest I offered them several durable chrome plated copies of my own autograph, offering as a gift my leading papier-mâché mastodon with blue suede tusks, but was left with silent rejection by the crew who left this advice behind: The combination of blue suede tusks and pink cupcake icing is the sign that you should become a pediatric nurse working in a maternity ward where the colors designating gender are also pink and blue.

THE CONDUIT

A man who's been stabbed in the heart, at the edge of a pipe, crawls inside it to live with the wound.

Moving down the windy concrete tunnel, listening to his arteries drain, he leaves a red carpet for the assailant's knife -

Millennial scorpion stinging itself drowning in cesspools of regeneration.

Huge, wide, longer than all seeing memory -

The pipe sparkles with light, twinkling with blood hitting the cold air -

The man looks inward, in quest of warmth, passing torn valves in a network of tubes -

From waning capillary to enlarged vein geysering woundward, the assailant has left the pipe as a memorial to his crime and victim, paying tribute with a spare part, in lieu of tubes torn.

The man builds a valve mid-pipe with sheets of dried blood, to impede his death.

In honor of the sacrificial kill, the ancestors of the victim and assailant line up in rows facing each other, linking pinkies in a twilight square dance.

The ancestors defy the order of time, choosing dance partners from non-overlapping lifetimes—intimate fleeting anachronisms linking pinkies across time - cosmic gene pools intermingling, remote family trees of lineage intertwine, rumbling destinies crisscross antlers - out-of-wedlock orphans catch milkweed motes of unknown forebears flying in the winds -

A dance caller shouts from sunburnt ashes of police reports of the crime, interspersed with incantatory testimony of twisted fallen witnesses silenced by the omniscient pipe.

Swing your partner, pipe-cave-mission-trillion souls are finding fission - making the wound get real sore - the guilty conscience wants some more - tinder pipe in a morning mist - starfish pinky make a fist -

Aorta forms and diagrams fleeting light makes April scram - ventricle snow - do-si-do -

The landscape surrounding the pipe hums with first and last breaths - repeating life cycles with relentless cicada buzz -

First last breaths twirling into a starfish-flaming with water broken cradle splinters from ancestral childhoods converging - seer and seen a spiral of babies lighting tornado fires - glowing starfish wreathed in memorial cradle splinter embers -

Chrysalis tinder pipe blowing cave mouths through bedrock riddling the Earth's core with molten birth certificate lava -

The ancestors' wedding rings looping in endless chains - jingling wind chimes celebrating unions, separations, departings, ecstatic cries of copulating millions crystallizing in orgies of glacial snow folk drilling each other with crooked-carrot-capillary divining rods - sad roots of the broken forgotten smelling the remembered -

Torrents of ancestral ego dust scattering across the tangible world vanishing down the pipe, warming the crawling man bleeding inward -

Patellas of killer and kill ossify in a drop of morning dew on a blade of crab grass, becoming a knee-rock of giant wishbone -

The man looks further inward, confronting each of his ancestors and his assailant's ancestors face to face -

Torrential eye contact with a trillion causing an avalanche of accomplices to face the original wound -

Square dancers passing through the man's body, slowing his crawl, making his path oblique - milkweed lint glazing capillary antlers -

The random chaos of transpersonal memory erupting -

The crawling man's toe-trampled heart riddled with dance slipper footprints causing him to somersault briefly -

Hidden enemy remoras posing as friends stick to the rolling man's limbs - sparks of neural synapse fire giving him momentum -

Mulch piles full of oracle eternity spill swill of ego dust - Poop chute-parachute-somersault-sleep-ventricle snow do-si-do -

Crude oil of raw vision a crying hyena jaw chewing windy concrete tunnel edges - seer and seen rotate endless eyes in the primordial socket -

Lightning striking the mass heartbeat of merged accomplices linked to the crime by the knife - Ritual stabbings going down in history as nonchalant pedestrian bloodlettings for masses of victims resigned to their fates -

The tip of the assailant's knife rising on the eastern horizon at the end of the tunnel, anticipating the cuts of a new day -

Millennial scorpion orphans stinging linked pinky tips with methodical relentless grace -

The red carpet for the assailant's knife coagulating into a pyramid of dance slippers muzzling ravenous infant hyenas salivating for a taste of the crawling man -

At the mid-pipe valve, the man looks outward, torrential eye contact with a trillion piercing the original wound, taking a panoramic sweep across the random chaos of transpersonal memory gone berserk -

Kamikaze pilots get reborn in the lonesome candle flame on a baby's first birthday cake -

Countries sacrificing their souls for honor get redeemed in a gallstone in the belly of a shark -

The first opposable starfish thumb grips the first lollipop given to a boy by a barber after a first haircut -

Hidden enemy remoras play ring around the rosy, mocking the grieving relatives of the victim, getting dizzy spinning on merry-go-rounds of petrified wood - a chorus of birds sing to the tune of the trickle of the man's arteries draining - heirs to the knife molt, flying through the sun -

The mute speak. The spastic sing. The humble and the lofty become Siamese twins.

Gluttons knit mittens for infant hyenas -

Codpieces of ancient fencers become virile timeless buoys floating in the ocean 2,000 miles from land -

Starfish flames in lieu of torn heart valves celebrate the chaos of memory in a beachcomber's periwinkle shell -

A tangent of the crawling man recedes into a rural backwoods, seeing his fifteen year old hick grandmother wrestling with an old mossback snapping turtle of an unknown forebear - The fleeting crescent of a cross-generational affair waxes on the man's irises with lucidity warming stiffening eyelids. The faded, yellowed, crumpled Dear John letter written by the assailant's great great great grandmother, to the victim's great great great great great great grandson looms across his vision with the magnitude of a crucial turning point in history - the awkward hesitant cadences of the Dear John Letter intoning in the assailant's great great great grandmother's ancient but girlish voice reverberates throughout the pipe - rustling the mid-pipe valve - ravenous packs of hyenas in the vanishing point at the end of the tunnel smell the pungent chest wound, seeing the man as ripe vulnerable prey, but the intensity of the anachronistic cross-generational broken affair scares the hyenas away - high pitched screech of the assailant's great great great grandmother's girlish voice echoing painfully in retreating hyena ears.

First last breath cicada buzz of crime replenishing and exonerating itself. Cosmic gene pools sift curds and whey. The contagion of the assailant's guilty conscience infecting the masses of pinky linked square dancers. Heirs to the assailant's knife coalesce fates - drinking at the watering hole of the original wound. Ventricle snow-do-si-do -

Accomplices linked to the crime by the knife become

dwindling cogs in the sacrifice – Ventricle snow do-si-do -

Accomplices linked to the crime by cosmic gene pools mixing become dwindling cogs in the sacrifice - Ventricle snow-do-si-do -

Kamikaze accomplices vanishing into the original wound become dwindling cogs in the sacrifice—Ventricle snow-do-si-do-

Cold tear hills of guilty conscience rust the assailant's knife lying on a muddy urban embankment near the edge of the windy concrete tunnel - killers and kills anonymous for generations vanish in the omniscient memorial.

The fallen assailant, embedded in the memorial, dangles a stabbing hand from a fissure in the arc of pipe above the crawling man.

The assailant's hand glistens with maple syrup dripping from every grandma's homemade waffles. Blessed with homespun goodness, the hand is at peace, as heirs to the knife stab new victims in the heart. Having paid tribute with a spare part in lieu of tubes torn, the tranquil assailant's hand glows with stalactites of grandma's maple syrup hanging off elongated digits striated with country butter churned by rustic maidens.

The sweet shining assailant's hand overshadows the light at the end of the tunnel sparkling digits pointing in myriad directions - indented squares of every grandma's homemade waffles lovingly skewered on overgrown spiraling finger nails.

The man looks up at the hand, whirling vortex of waffles coming into sharp focus in his vision, tempting him with the prospect of a meal - the hand gently summons the man to rise, walk erect, facing all fear and uncertainty. With divine sign language an index finger nail says stop crawling - a ring finger says stop somersaulting - a thumb says prolong your life - a middle finger says come eat - a pinky says rise up.

The man gazes at the hand, slowly rising, hidden enemy remoras spiral up and down his legs as he clutches the gaping wound in his chest, the drama of his ascent slowed down by swarms of ancestral ego dust prowling. He listens to the passionate tumult of manic ancestral swarms giggling with merriment and mischief as they try to pull the rising man back down to the pipe floor, shackling his arms and legs with their wedding ring chain spiral—bombarding him with conflicts of past unions split apart.

Torrential eye contact of ancestral ego dust mobs trying, with the bullying force of numbers, to stare him down, crippling him back to a crawl with hard retinal intimidation - trillions of sad angry faces superimpose, blurring into each other, bombarding him with minefields of conflicting emotion - clever tricks turning banal as a mediocrity far back in someone's lineage showers him with zealous pamphlets extolling the virtues of crawling.

THE BALL

A line projecting from a man's forehead is all oiled up, slippery and infinite, flowing from a far off source, inching backwards on his pate and vanishing against the horizon in the opposite direction.

He cups the line to his ear, listening to the sound of taut sputtering machinery operating in unison. He then follows the line to its terminus or wellspring, traveling by foot until coming to a swiveling metallic ball looming at the center of a city.

The man stands before the ball watching his line run through the walls far above him. The ball is threaded up with a network of hairlines projecting outward in all directions from the hub, octopus style.

The lines run to where they are rooted in the foreheads of men with varying degrees of baldness who move freely, untethered by their threads which they pull while going about their daily business, keeping the ball swivelling with each and every movement.

The man, never passing the others of this rooted set on his way to the ball, walks around it banging on the tinny walls, finding the entrance hatch and pulling his line in with him.

The interior apparatus of the parietal structure, or, jargon aside—the innards of the big ball; is a huge control room with rows of floodlights lining a curved ceiling and circular walls all speckled over with tiny openings through which the lines run in and out.

At the center of the room, wedged between floor and ceiling, is a grillwork partition where a cadre of line operators are maneuvering the lines through the openings in the walls as they unwind from slow, moderate, and rapid receding spindles and run through bottles of Cure-Via-Cause oil.

The rooted set go bald on this oil conveyed to their pates via the lines which shorten as they absorb them, getting pulled towards and into the ball by the line operators.

The ball is a generic umbrella toupee; causing covering and hence curing the bald, who become line operators, causing the baldness of others. The lines are the heavenly elixir of all good men. Overlapping genetically & commercially so that infinitely receding generations willing to do business, can get a roof over their heads and benefit from the cure.

The man steps through the glistening webbed network; feeling his line well up inside him, oozing in through a cranial pore, soothing his whole head and face the way cool tonics and aftershaves do.

He watches the operators maneuvering the lines through the openings in the walls. Some operators sit at tables adjacent to the grillwork where they scribble down jargon in little pamphlets, while others thread newly wound lines through bottle and wall openings, pulling them out of the ball and rooting them in the foreheads of the populace.

Still other operators stand facing the inner walls of the ball, pressing their eyes against the openings and peering out of them as though through telescopes, scanning the terrain of the city until spotting the rooted set moving towards the ball.

Sometimes several days pass before even one is spotted, while waiting, the operators watch the distant traffic and crowds of pedestrians as well as an occasional mischievous child who throws an egg at the ball and then hides, watching from a distance to see if the operators will emerge to come looking for him or her.

Sooner or later, the rooted set come into view, one by one at intervals, going bald simultaneously at different rates; the operators pulling them towards and into the ball gently, without tethered coercion, guiding them in through the entrance hatch.

As the man threads a line through an oil bottle, he watches another operator shackling a rapid receding spindle in rubber encasing so it won't get out of his control, snapping its line in mid-process, the man at the other end vanishing into the city with a broken thread trailing from his forehead in the wind.

THE UNICYCLIST

Insidious clusters of duck-billed platypus eggs are multiplying in a unicycling nomad's scrotum.

Via the mass of eggshells permeable, the fluid nest of platypi nibble on the delicate hors d' oeuvres of their host's testicles, stretching the envelope to thinnest transparency and the tense verge of bursting.

Shining through the scrotal sac, twinkling in stars far and near, swarms of bluish eggs bulge over the saddle of the nomad's unicycle making pedaling most difficult-

But pedal he must–with relentless prudent toe-tips, he-she-it, is the yoked transitional martyr caught between species, without precedent or family tree, the first and last of its kind, bereft of destination and cause, ever so careful not to crush the precious eggs against the saddle while riding up and down endless hills strewn with buttercups and clover.

Leg muscles bulging, arms flailing the wind with Dodo bird wing inutility—two left hands twirling a long tall back scratcher built from stolen shepherds' staffs fixed end to end with morning dew glue–

The nomad pedals furiously, never sleeping stopping or looking backwards; two left hands miming smiles of waking dreams for swallows swooping down pecking kisses of levity upon his chapped muttony frown, saddened and dulled by the uniform passing view of wayward shepherdless sheep, aimless melting forms of boredom trickling down far off mole holes riddling the vast expanse of hills.

Where pristine sameness reigns, winter fall and summer are fibs of rogue mischief, the folly of phantom seasons carved in the far ends of the back scratcher by stray shepherds' children orphaned by their fathers in pursuit of stolen staffs.

Throughout the hills, an endless spring asserts a timeless calm, lush with new beginnings, every buttercup has just bloomed, the fresh scent of clover wafts up from forward turning unicycle wheel as new eggs join swarms of brethren spontaneously–

Windswept facial pores tornadoing sweat off his brow–zigzagging in fierce rivulets through valleys between tightly crowding egg bumps pressing the limits of taut elastic skin–back scratcher answering a primordial itch–steaming fragile but invincible scrotum swelling up into a mountain thrusting into clouds–

The nomad is cloaked in the imperial shadows of glory–protruding with Portuguese-man-of-war severity–reflecting violent blue hues in spinning wheel spokes–

Binding monotreme umbra fusing he-she-it and platypus into one.

Across the hilly landscape the penumbra engulfs the cog adrift in its wanton life cycle–

Portuguese hors d'oeuvre-of war–ballooning into a host of infinite generosity.

Ecstatic cryptozoologists crawl out of the hills to classify the new species but it eludes their grasp–

Quack doctors with miracle cures, carrying weighty tomes entitled "Elephantiasis of the scrotum, the laurels of a lofty masculinity" are swallowed up by the umbra before they can dupe their patient, naïve but inscrutable.

Seductive wood nymphs try to extract the eggs orgasmically, but fail to arouse the lust of the monkish unicyclist and are sent back to charm school—

Lachrymose tailors design elegant costumes too small for the nomad, poorly contoured to the ever expanding scrotum bursting through impeding seams, threads, buttons and lace; tailors drowning in tears shed over abandoned sartorial carrion littering the hills, cast off by the nomad pedaling naked and free.

Oviparous losers wait for the nomad to lay the eggs in honor of their legacy but vanish with disappointment—

Ovoviviparous dreamers erased by their own dust bum around forever to never hear the cracking of eggs hatching—

Viviparous demons rejoice with parthenogenetic tricksters mutually validated by the nomad's triumphant existence—

The nomad cycles in darkness and light—following a random feral route beyond the limits of time and exhaustion—gelded by the cosmos in flux—the eunuch ushering in the continuum of a new breed—harsh winds tornadoing sweat off his brow—watering the buttercups and clover.

Via the mass of eggshells permeable, ravenous platypi bills suck up and regurgitate partially digested iotas of manhood, thus radically increasing and decreasing testosterone levels; every seven hill climbs, the nomad alternating between caricatured polarities of virility and effeminacy at regular intervals.

The nomad uttering cacophonous gibberish of resonant baritone interspersed with squeaky falsetto: AAAAOOOO-iiiiiiii-I—ih!!—ihhhhhhh! OOOAHIOU—ihhh!

Trembling the mole, haunting the swallow, making the heart of the cryptozoologist beat fast with ecstatic expectation—

Dispersing stray shepherds' children carving fibs of winter fall and summer in the far ends of the back scratcher—tingling the buttercups and clover....

The nomad built the back scratcher during virile phases, forcefully wrestling staffs from the tight grips of raging shepherds. He showed off for the nymphs, basking in idyllic glory; pedaling resolutely, unicycle wheel balanced and firm, back scratcher clenched heroically between mossy wind warped teeth—

Two left arms subduing shepherds in full nelsons, hurling them towards distant future stars, morning dew gluing the fresh staff booty to the far ends of the back scratcher.

Two left arms subduing the fresh mold of cryptozoologists and quack doctors in half nelsons, thus erasing discovery of the new species and silencing medical sophistry—

Coquettish nymphs graduate from charm school with honors, enrapt by the nomad's wrestling powers; charming nymphs lactating and soothing the motherless nomad older than the hills, squirting he-she-it with infatuated milk—quenching a lusty thirst every seven virile hill climbs—

Fickle nymphs fizzling at the cusp of the manly wane of the nomad turning into a monkish limp-wristed sissy.

Predatory mobs of raging shepherds intent on retrieving their staffs, roam the hills stalking the nomad during vulnerable phases of effeminacy—

If the shepherds ever get close enough to tackle the nomad, he twirls the back scratcher counterclockwise, manically cycling in circles so fast until magically vanishing into the chasm of chapped muttony frown, emitting a deafening high pitched falsetto screech—two left hands of the waking dream miming all the shepherds' deepest fears—frightful sign language and piercing screech knocking shepherds off their feet, rolling down hill and slithering vanquished down far off mole holes.

The nomad thus cementing his dominion, emerging from the safety of the defensive trick, sissydom waning, giving way to toughness, the voice of a thousand pubertys cracking, deepening and tingling the buttercups and clover.

Deep in their shells, the platypi are hypnotized into memory and song by the relentless pace of the nomad's cycling. The up and down rhythm of pedaling legs causing a faint chorus of tiny platypi bills to tap inner shells in harmony—singing the refrain of the last Dodo bird chirp trailing off into silence—mourning the inutility of the Dodo birds' wing—celebrating the Dodo birds' flight home to roost in hosts on a distant future star.

The hills tremble gently with masses of lulled footsteps of stray shepherds' children, orphans of eternal spring, breaking into a somnolent gallop, driven towards the distant chorus of platypi bills tapping inner shells in harmony.

Policing deep in the nomad's shadow an umbra-warden smothered in costume carrion oversees a chain gang of crying tailors shackled ankle to ear with broken threads, seams, zippers, buttons and lace—

The eggs continue to multiply beyond time, chimerical fauna never hatching, embarking on an eternal incubation and the scourge of ovoviviparous bums erased by their own dust—

Platypi feasting at the banquet of Portuguese-hors d'oeuvre-of-war—scrotum ballooning into a host of infinite generosity—

Swarms of bluish eggs bulge over the saddle of the nomad's unicycle far and wide, making pedaling most difficult—

But pedal he must.

The yoked transitional martyr caught between species, the first and last of its kind, ever so careful to remain undiscovered and not crush the precious eggs against the saddle.

Safe in their niche, the chorus of eggs grows louder, ringing violent blue hues in the nomad's ears—

The nomad cycling to the rhythm of the platypi tapping inner egg shells, reverberating throughout his body in flux—

Two left arms flailing the wind with Dodo bird wing inutility, groping towards an aerodynamic majesty—

Two left hands glowing with sinistral clairvoyance, twirling the back scratcher glistening in the orange grey dawn with morning dew glue, answering a primordial itch—

Imperial umbra reaching above endless hills, engulfing stars far and near—

Echoes of platypi bills tapping inner shells in harmony, tingling the buttercups and clover.

THE EMBEZZLER

A fugitive embezzler lies inside a couch with a spring stuck through his body like a skewer. Flanked by the curlicue bars of his shishkebab cell, he cries and sweats in atonement, hoping to whitewash his police record to which the couch could be added as a footnote.

But via the emission of his criminal fluids the blue-green virtue of his copper addiction is born; verdigris forms on the spring where it runs in and out of the embezzler's body.

The spring's shell of liquid green courses through his veins, and the memory of his life on the lam in quest of bank notes is eclipsed by a toxin-bound life of sedentary prostration.

In a burst of virtuous glory he slides off his spring and goes through withdrawal, seeing a fleeting image of Abraham Lincoln pass before his eyes.

Upon returning to the spring he feels like an earnest young boy lying along the beams of a log cabin, reading by the dull green light on his habit—the tiny images and patent numbers on each and every spring as though they held the rebus of a mint vault.

While lost in the dreams of the lives of the men on pennies, the embezzler's copper addiction grows—the blue-green crust spreading across the expanse of couch springs, encasing them in an interior sulfate slipcover.

From one end of the couch frame to the other, the network of verdigris coils is flickering like rows of festive mistletoe—the harbingers of many a successful Christmas bank robbery.

THE INK DEVICE

In order to isolate the spirit of unrequited love, a collector of personal mail has separated stacks of love letters into categories according to the degrees of their emotional content.

In a small room the letters hang from rows of pipes running between opposite walls. From the ceiling above, a watering system of spigots is wetting the letters; the ink dripping off them and running through filters and gutters which remove all impurities before the ink drains into little bottles on the floor.

On each bottle the collector has written the dates the letters were stolen and the names of the addressees.

He appends little pamphlets to the bottles which explain how to re-enact the circumstances which caused the letters to be written so that an identical rewriting can be done.

The collector packages the bottles and pamphlets with the blank letters and mails them back to the letter writers. He paces back and forth across the room, hitting a crumpled envelope with his foot, waiting for a plaintiff's response.

He then retires to a corner of the room, listening to the spray of spigots, gurgle of filters and gutters and the relentless drip drop of ink draining into little black bottles while gazing up at rows of dripping love letters in various stages of erasure.

The Ink Device is located in an office building in a large city.

The collector leaves his room at night when all the office workers have gone home. Like a coal miner hermit engulfed in halos of ink drizzle, he journeys through rows of offices on every floor, foraging through the desk drawers of secretaries, finding fragments of secret office romances and effusive thank you notes penned in ornate purplish script on perfumed paper with floral patterned edges.

During his nightly letter raids, he is intoxicated by the sound of the Ink Device flowing in unison with the plumbing, faucets, toilets and gurgling water coolers throughout the building. He pauses to listen to the footsteps of the Concise-Paced-Effusion Company, an agency of emotional controller-spies moving through the dark building, encircling the Ink Device room, waiting to catch the collector and lend him their relatives' personal mail at a loan shark's rate.

The Concise-Paced-Effusion agents try to prevent the collector from leaving the room so he will have to rely on them to get new love letters. They threaten to report him to the board of health, for his water wasting full blast spigots drenching ornate letters of wealthy verbose decadents who lived the high life, free of pedestrian concerns. The collector presses his ear against an office wall listening to an apocalyptic vision of all romantic emotional written matter washing over him like a tidal wave of transient love affairs all remembered at once.

In apartment buildings all over the city, the collector's plaintiffs write subpoenas with the ink from the little black bottles anonymously received in the mail.

ARBITRATION, AT GOO...

Two continents are linked by a pipeline through which liquid babyfood flows, linking the respective populations by their diet.

The inhabitants of both continents have regressed to a permanent condition of teething after many generations of a homogenized diet of soft babyfood requiring no chewing.

Hovering on the cusp of toothless obsolescence, the inhabitants are stuck at the stage of cutting teeth because the babyfood vacillates between chewable and potable consistencies—the goo thickening gradually, returning to a liquid state—only to thicken again with the regularity of seasons.

The continents are isolated cul-de-sacs at opposite ends of the pipeline, which is the only source of contact between the two land masses.

The diet which the two continents share keeps them ignorant of each other. The goo is an impenetrable wall between the two sets of inhabitants who blame their teething pain on each other.

A teething pain cold war develops between the two sets of inhabitants.

To resolve the teething pain cold war, swarms of arbitrators swim back and forth through the pipeline, moving against the swift currents of yellow goo like anthropomorphic salmon equipped with goo-proof backpacks filled with rubber teething rings.

The arbitrators swim for long months at goo—semi-aquatic transients constantly passing each other while swimming towards opposite ends of the pipeline.

The arbitrators emerge from the edges of the pipeline—dripping yellow blobs awkwardly unloading backpacks, hurling slippery fistfuls of teething rings into crowds of disgruntled inhabitants crowding around the edges of the pipeline.

Some of the inhabitants are placated by the teething rings, while others reject them as a ruse, interrogating the arbitrators with questions about their enemy.

Still other inhabitants blame the arbitrators for their teething pain, claiming that they maintain their teething condition in a fixed permanent state, thwarting the need for chewing by swimming back and forth through the goo, keeping it forever soft and preventing it from hardening into a chewable consistency.

The arbitrators can stay on dry land for short periods of time only, otherwise their coats of dripping babyfood will rapidly harden in the open air, stiffening their limbs, encasing them in inflexible shells crippling them in immobility.

During their short periods of time on dry land, the arbitrators make rapid speeches, interviewing the inhabitants, answering their questions in a cursory manner, refuting their accusations—a chorus of voices slowing down and trailing off as the goo starts to harden on the arbitrators' lips which stop moving . . .

The arbitrators dive back into the pipeline without resolving the cold war. They vanish beneath the surface of the goo and start swimming to opposite ends of the pipeline as the inhabitants complain of their fragmentary inadequate diplomacy.

On one of the continents a rogue arbitrator stays on dry land.

The rogue, encased in dried goo armor, wanders stiffly with unbending arms and legs; a mute yellow mummy ablaze with burning rubber teething rings adorning his armor like melting birthday candles.

Axe wielding mobs of inhabitants scapegoat the rogue, trying to hack him to pieces—axe blades resounding in a series of dull thuds on the iron hard exoskeleton of goo. The flaming rubber teething rings blunting the axe blades after repeated blows.

Deep in his goo chamber, the rogue listens to the remote axe blades chopping like the faint taps of a woodpecker far in the distance.

THE UN-PATENTED UNIVERSE

A pragmatic-visionary inventor has stolen a poetic-kernel inventor's idea and developed it.

In the throes of a plagiaristic mating season comes a hybrid-germ-batter ripening from the stratagems of a wide ranging mind.

A scattered and vague notion conceived during a pang of inspiration drifts through galaxies, snowballing into a many-sided composite idea applicable for ending class struggle, starving the overfed, and annihilating all alien enemies.

In the shadows of an un-patented universe the inventors stand engulfed in debate.

The pragmatic visionary inventor claims that he rescued the idea from a decorative fate; weaning the bud of its limitations and delivering it into the nursery of infinitely expanding ideas.

The poetic-kernel inventor claims that in his quest for diverse clutter, his rival has made a jerry-built contraption, all glitter and no utility.

To which the pragmatic-visionary inventor replies: you gave birth without responsibility, so I took up where you left off, what you begin, I am fated to finish in a grand scheme where the complex swallow up and build on the foundations of the simple...where personal zones of credit merge as unequal victims grow dependent in an unwilling collaboration.

In the throes of a plagiaristic mating season, snowballs of hybrid germ batter blossom, drifting through galaxies of larger and lesser minds mating.

THE HERMIT

My tree is tall and hollow. I hide in a grotto of roots in the trunk, half buried in dirt and rotting wood fiber.

When I want to remember my past life in the outside world, I look up at a thin bar of light coming through a small hole above me.

A bird's nest is stuck between a crevice of bark near the bar of light. The faint rustle of feathers is the sign of the bird passing through the hole while returning to or leaving the nest.

My head is covered with an accretion of bird droppings which has slowly become a helmet growing an iota thicker each time the bird drops on me. The helmet has begun to extend down the sides of my head, sealing over my ears, drowning out the barking pursuit of Bloodhound-Stigmata encroaching in the distance.

I am resigned to dining on grubs and termites. This humble repast grossly offends my rarefied palate pining desperately for a Crêpe Suzette or Linzertorte.

Fate is the absence of luxury but the impunity of Mephistopheles The Doppelgänger.
The fake twin contains all crimes.

Blame rests squarely on the shoulders of the insignificant other; the fall guy and eternal alibi stooped in servitude, acting as a human shield, buffering nosy inroads of the Bloodhound-Stigmata.

My grin bears twins in infinity. My twins mutate unculled triplets and wood lice get stuck between my teeth, humbling my culinary pretense. Triplets and twins repent! Triplets and twins pay tree rent!

Cog in the fire machine! resurrect! vivisect! resurrect! vivisect!

I keep track of time by measuring the minute gradations in my helmet's thickness with a notched root torn from the grotto with my teeth. Gnawing on the root in the darkness I have covered it end to end with rows of notches—the root turning into a functional Braille ruler which I read with my fingertips in the darkness. I hold the root against the edges of my helmet near my cheeks, neck, and forehead, measuring the distances between my skin and the top strata of my helmet.

Doppelgänger? I am willfully lost beyond a mirage of unculled triplets under microscopes—the wild surgeon's scalpel is our cross to bear—wild surgeon's scalpel hoe! twin! hoe! cull! triplet! cull! Agriculture is the albatross of my insignificant other humbly gripping a laborer's hoe in callused hands, tending a little vegetable garden right outside my tree.

I mourn my fallen empire while looters grow rich off my pioneering spirit. My insignificant other furrows in the soil, poking runty carrots, oblivious to my whereabouts—hoe! twin! hoe!

I'm planning on issuing a battalion of rabid angels to blackmail the insignificant other into growing fields of poisonous mushrooms for our nemesis the Goody Goody Two Shoes.

The Goody Goody Two Shoes is the unculled mutant insubordinate chip off my insignificant other; an unwanted accidental triplet threatening our freedom at large.

I take into consideration that every time the bird drops on me, falling down the length of the hollow tree, the droppings do not always land on my head. For each one of the bird's misfirings, I make a note of the demerit, by subtracting a notch from the root, running it gingerly between my molars until feeling a tiny loose wood bump on my tongue. In my dogged quest for precision, I have calculated that two inches of bird droppings accumulate on my head per year.

According to the laws governing the symbiosis of victim and victimizer, royalties are my entitlement, but they haven't been forthcoming. Sacrifice has its place, Resurrect. Vivisect.

The Goody Goody Two Shoes is too dumb to know that my insignificant other's hoe is the incognito instrument of an invisible surgeon, who, through subterfuge, enables my experimental living tissue to fall between the interstice of the law. Guinea pig hailstones in vacuum packed tin cans fall from the sky; my insignificant other hits the cans with the hoe, playing solitaire stickball.

New notches of measurement are carved in the root with finger and toe nails. Big toe nails for deep notches, pinky nails for shallow notches, index fingernails for moderate notches. Spare demerit notch bumps are pouched in my navel marsupial style, blurring my fingerprints—hexing the Bloodhound-Stigmata.

Sometimes Mass Murderers Anonymous comes knocking tree to tree, soliciting donations, holding out makeshift beggar's cups made from emptied guinea pig hailstone cans they've stolen out of the sky, before the poor cans could have a chance of hitting the ground, the Goody Goody Two Shoes, or my insignificant other. If I could collect all the donations of Mass Murderers Anonymous, they might add up to a fraction of my royalties due.

You want me to confess? My lust is thwarted. The Goody Goody Two Shoes opposes sex before marriage, preventing my prostitute from visiting me in my tree. The Goody Goody Two Shoes has hung a swing on the largest branch of my tree. My grotto sways slightly, tiny networks of fissures deep in the strata of my helmet shift seismic minutiae when the Goody Goody Two Shoes swings back and forth knitting my chastity diapers with righteous indignation. The chastity diapers prevent me from breeding. When my prostitute gets wind of the reflections of the chastity diaper sparkling forth rays of my involuntary celibacy, she runs through the forest in the opposite direction from my tree.

I must breed for I am the Phoenix of my people. Resurrect! Vivisect! Long live the Guppy/Barracuda who cancel each other out, eluding the fisherman's nets!

The Goody Goody Two Shoes is trying to be clever, by embroidering on my chastity diapers the phrase "AERIAL RECONNAISSANCE OF DEPOSED FUGITIVE KINGS." Dangling off the safety pin of the diaper is a little glow-in-the-dark cartoon of me in full-helmet regalia, standing on my head on the top branch of my tree, waving SOS flags at Bloodhound-Stigmata search planes, flying overhead combing the forest for me.

The silly pranks of the Goody Goody Two Shoes do not scare me. It was my fate to profit off the misfortune of others, so I could build a ladder to the research cradle in the sky with bones from an entire species I almost made extinct. Die Wahrheit ist ein Geheimnis. There will be no misused and stolen guinea pig hailstones, Resurrect—Vivisect—Circumspect—for now, I bide my time, a mute for my cause, tolerating my predicament of bequeathing upon myself the albatross of the unculled triplet vulgarly advertising our mutating selves to the world.

I can't decide if the Goody Goody Two Shoes or my insignificant other will take the blame if I'm ever caught by the Bloodhound-Stigmata. I travel to the future on a thin bar of moonlight, in five years my helmet will be as wide as the diameter of the tree trunk—the helmet growing into a mausoleum headdress which will get stuck between the inner walls of the tree. Fate is pain without repentance.

Once, I had big dreams of stuffing the bird and putting it inside the tiny cuckoo clock I carved at the tip of my notched root. With arrogance I thought I could usurp the bird by shaking the tree, causing the eggs to fall from the nest, smashing on top of my helmet, the vanquished babybirds adorning my headdress like the chevrons on the military uniform worn in my youth. I have grown to accept the mausoleum-headdress with grim abandon. Grandiose dreams of stuffing babybird beaks with spare demerit notch bumps, in simulation of stuffing apples in suckling pig mouths, have been cast to the winds with pageantry and elegant clothes.

The mausoleum-headdress will still my absconding retirement plans, bringing my intense static secrecy to an end. Not a bad fate after running half my life.

We exhausted the flesh to break free of the bone -

A bone to abscond will thwart a Bloodhound-Stigmata –

Baby chevrons hidden in Linzertortes will be bones of temptation for persuers -

Break free of the bone riddling Crêpe Suzettes with fusillades of spare demerit notch bumps on misty nights -

To exhaust the flesh pulverize the bone of the Bloodhound-Stigmata -

Die Endlösung ist eine ewige Aufgabe -

Wir sind überhaupt nicht schuldig -

To catch a deposed king swaddle him in Crêpe-Chevron-Suzettes -

When a machine goes up in flames donate your grotto to science -

Die Wissenschaft ist unbestechlich -

Chevron-Stigmata break free of Linzer-Bone exhaust - Linzer-bumps in Crêpe roots bring notches of demerit to Torte-Suzettes -

Spare demerit notch bumps pouched in machine will make marsupials hide fingerprints in Stigmata belly buttons -

Deposed kings reenact pageantry in a grotto of roots - Grub machine Grub-grub machine grub-grub war—grub war-root—root-war—root is the better part of precision -

Precision is roots of demerit bumps in guinea pig tin cans -

Die Menschenversuche müssen unbedingt genau sein -

Continent to continent—across oceans—ocean to tree—tree to land—land to bog—dull government scalpel knives rusting in a peat bog—

Bogged down in fading newspaper headlines of a king at large—King looming larger than the mirage beyond the microscope—

Tall tree tales do not a cryptic ghost make—demerit selves are protean fakes—

Protean ghosts carve a stigmata in the bark—Protean ghost kings are waiting for a thin bar of moonlight—

The Hermit continues his cryptic soliloquy, overcompensating for his poverty with lofty memories of haute cuisine and the martial grandeur of fallen political machines, referring to himself as a king in the third person.

The lofty thoughts are interspersed with fear of his persuers, shifting mutable identities, phantom whores denied, and qualms about the bird's control of his fate.

The jumbled thoughts and memories, distorted and fragmented from years of isolation, blend in a bitter cacophony of logorrhea; relentless voice echoing up and down the thick walls of the tree, causing the nested bird to cock its head quizzically.

The hermit's isolation induced hallucinations of his distant crimes have materialized in the form of guinea pig hailstone cans, which are his diced, vacuum packed victims returning to him in streamlined cylinders raining down from the cradle of pure research in the sky. The hailstones threaten the fugitive anonymity of the hermit, but are viewed as wayward trophies bestowed upon a cruel zealot; perverse laurels for a guilt-free conscience.

Er hat kein Gewissen. Es gibt keine Vergangenheits-bewältigung.

The hermit rolls over in his grotto, leaning his helmet against the inside walls of the tree trunk, scraping chalky grayness of cranial exoskeleton against termite-riddled wood. He drums his fingers up and down the notches of his root in the darkness—

Phantom marsupials hatching from spare demerit notch bumps in his navel. His strong, indomitable will remains free of the senility of old age, but he is tinged with a stoic arrogance and lofty sense of entitlement. His regal attitude ridiculously contrasting with his humble state of ruin.

Ruined but free, the hermit was once a Doctor. By accident he became a fugitive, on the run for most of his adult life. The war torn fallen government which once employed the hermit, rewarded him for experimentation on enemies of the state.

A chevron was added to his uniform for every incongruous mutilation of flesh and degradation of spirit. He was crowned with new heights of glory with the long screams of each slow, agonizing kill. The rigor mortis of each butchered subject elevated the hermit's rank to the zenith of the cradle of pure research in the sky.

He who had carte blanche was only fulfilling his lawful duties. He for whom medical malpractice was an understated euphemism, forever washed his hands clean of blood, running from new laws condemning him for his past deeds. Exiled from his country, he fled across oceans and continents, to remain free.

In order to permanently trick and elude his persuers, the hermit made a pawn which he vivisected with a hoe blade, resourcefully whittling the crude garden tool with stones turning it into a makeshift surgeon's scalpel.

He performed cosmetic surgery on the pawn with ruthless precision, surgically remodeling him into the insignificant other, an identical twin of himself.

The hermit cautiously hacked out the insignificant other's tongue so he would remain mute if captured, thus preventing the possibility of damaging testimony about the hermit to leak before a court of law.

The Goody Goody Two Shoes was born ignis fatuus; unculled triplet wantonly mutating from surgical scraps of flesh flying randomly off the jagged scalpel blade during the operation.

The insignificant other howled in agony, sputtering in a harsh red wind of incisions, the surgeon's exacting hands dancing nimbly; frilly ruffles of Goody's bloomers widening in rippling spirals of dainty cloth lily pads around its legs; horizontal rows of ruffles materializing in manic flutters like the invisible beating of thousands of hummingbird wings. Amidst the mutating mayhem and transformation, the first idea for a chastity diaper had already formed in the Goody Goody Two Shoe's head long before the insignificant other's scars had begun to heal.

The insignificant other traveled in bondage with the hermit as he moved through an endless series of ephemeral jobs as hotel manager, store clerk, farmer and overseer of manual laborers. The hermit's identity changed with each new job. The jobs becoming more menial over time, until the hermit, bereft of authority, stopped working and began drifting, discarding all his belongings except his pawn, wandering into a remote forest never to return to civilization.

Deeper and deeper into the forest the hermit and his pawn traveled, The Goody Goody Two shoes trailing behind secretly; bloomer ruffles scraping against dense underbrush could not be heard above the chorus of humming insects rubbing their legs in song. Eventually, the discordant trio settled in a small clearing where the insignificant other was put to work gardening, and the hermit burrowed into the grotto of roots under his hollow tree, Goody hanging a swing on the largest branch of the tree, swinging and knitting chastity diapers.

The Bloodhound-Stigmata were bounty hunters, hoping to catch the hermit, bringing him to justice for a huge reward. The Bloodhound-Stigmata flew over the forest in search planes, scanning the treetops aerially, until they caught a glimpse of a glistening diaper reflecting in the sun and a huge knitting needle poking through the tree branches.

Landing their plane to investigate, they bushwhacked through the dense forest, carrying mug shots of the hermit, drinking tequila and eating snared rabbits skewered over campfires.

Upon reaching the clearing, the scenario before them appeared to be a hallucination induced from a daily diet of rabbit and tequila: Goody, prim and clean, knitted diapers diligently, swinging back and forth from a high tree branch, down below, the insignificant other, emaciated and filthy, hoeing and drooling from his tongue stump, inadvertently watering the garden with rivulets of saliva; pausing to bat a guinea pig hailstone can up to Goody with the hoe; Goody opening the can, holding flesh cubes between two knitting needles like chopsticks, eating the remnants of the hermit's victims, engaging in a proper cannibalism within acceptable bounds of culinary etiquette, Goody, careful not to soil its bloomers with oily juices from the rarefied meal; tossing the empty can down from the swing with haughty indifference, the can bouncing off the insignificant other and landing in the garden next to the tree. The pile of glistening chastity diapers next to the garden, a sculptural testament to the hermit's virtuous celibacy, the diapers were never actually worn, being too precious like an antique loveseat which had supreme decorative value, but was too delicate to be sat upon.

The Bloodhound-Stigmata quickly noticed the strong resemblance between the insignificant other and the hermit. They quickly captured the insignificant other mistaking him for the hermit. They handcuffed him, leading him out of the forest as Goody watched, continuing to knit methodically. Goody knew the truth but would not inform on the hermit, because it would violate the controlled routine-bound world the hermit created. If Goody were to tell the Bloodhound-Stigmata of the hermit's whereabouts, they might then put on the precious chastity diapers as work clothes, ruining the diapers while chopping the down the tree to capture the hermit, thus eliminating the tree branch from which Goody swung. Also, there was no guarantee that the Bloodhound-Stigmata would share their reward money with Goody after informing on the hermit. Much to Goody's chagrin, the leader of the Bloodhound-Stigmata triumphantly put on the diaper with "Aerial Reconnaissance of Deposed fugitive kings" embroidered on it with a glow in the dark cartoon of the hermit dangling off the safety pin.

Goody watched as the Bloodhound-Stigmata vanished into the forest underbrush, its favorite diaper flashing between trees as the leader bushwhacked away, the glowing cartoon of the hermit twirling on his hip with each rugged step and snap of twig.

The insignificant other was flown to a distant continent, brought to justice and found guilty of crimes he was a victim of.

Mute with drooling tongue stump before the court, the insignificant other was unable to defend himself against his prosecutors. The incriminating testimony about the hermit which could exculpate the insignificant other, remained stuck in painful gibberish—tongue stump wagging desperately—his spirit broken, traumatized by the surgery from which he was created—the insignificant other cried in murky confusion trying to remember clearly what was done to him by the hermit—struggling to articulate an intelligible word, his tears mixing with drool, covering his face with his hands as the prosecutors coldly issued a guilty verdict. The Bloodhound-Stigmata soon after getting their reward.

The insignificant other was executed for crimes he was a victim of. The fall guy and eternal alibi fulfilled the destiny the hermit designed him for. The pawn completed its life cycle. Resurrect. Vivisect. Circumspect. The complacent world hated and reviled the memory of the insignificant other, forever deceived; rows of mangled scapegoats receded into the horizon of their smug blindness. Conventional wisdom prevented the possibility of anyone considering that this was a case of mistaken identity. The far-fetched chance that the accused was a dupe of malleable putty from an elusive surgeon's scalpel, a pawn in the hands of deception, was considered absurdly ludicrous by the prudent body politic. Societies ebbed and flowed, governments fluctuated, ossified public opinions gathered dust, then momentum, the dried kernel of the insignificant other's severed tongue rolled across antiseptic horizons—a tastebud tumbleweed engulfing the pain of all seasons.

The hermit was forgotten, vanishing as intended, increment by increment; the bird dropped on his helmet, droppings slowly accreting into the mausoleum headdress filling the inside walls of the tree trunk, entombing the hermit.

All the trees of the forest burned to the ground, and the Goody Goody Two Shoes' ashes were heaped in a neat series of chastity diaper urns twinkling in the flames. Long after the hermit became ash in the flames, the hollow helmet of bird dung drifted through invisible fields of ashy dust—a fossil impervious to the erosion of time—

Time. Maker of wounds. Turning all extremities into seamless plateaus—rain, wind, and stardust swept around the helmet's rough contours, smoothing over the last notch bump indentation left by the root—forlorn remnants of exacting precision cast to oblivion—Monumental strata of bird dung—bedrock of Phoenix—the spirit of hearing sent forth an ear which cupped itself to the helmet's concavity, listening to the oceans of the world roaring in the bird shell.

VANITY

I was dead, lying inside an open marble coffin, as the mortician injected embalming fluid into my body with a syringe.

The inside of the coffin was lined with pink satin. I pulled at it with my fingers, looking up at the mortician as I spoke in a critical tone, "Well, what if the worms don't like this?"

The mortician pretended not to hear me. I stared at his syringe as it penetrated my skin. The embalming fluid felt cool as it rushed through my body, like a refreshing cold drink on a hot summer day after hiking above the tree line of a mountain summit.

Again, I looked up at the mortician and spoke, "But I don't want to be preserved! And how are the worms going to get into this marble box after you close it? And what if the worms don't like the taste of the embalming fluid–just like children who won't eat their vegetables?

The mortician looked at me smugly as he spoke in a lofty philosophical tone, "My friend, you are addicted to sensual pleasures. You are so attached to your own gratifications that I don't believe you are ready for the spiritual plane."

I sat up in my coffin waving my arms about as I spoke, "But you're depriving me of my natural processes and desires! I had wished to view my body as it decomposed and to photograph each stage of the process." I held my expensive camera aloft so the mortician could see it.

"Surely, this is not an impractical idea, is it? Surely it can't be! My needs are no different from parents who photograph their children at different stages of maturity so they can look back with warm sentiment and see how all has changed!"

The mortician stood motionless, stern and reproving with arms crossed, shaking his head saying, "So vain, so very, very vain."

THE PARALLEL BETWEEN THE CAKE AND THE TAIL

A groom who is about to be married is polishing the pink plastic flamingos on his manicured front lawn. After a long time, that all knowing quality indigenous to lawn statuary reminds him not to be late to his wedding. When he arrives at the church the atmosphere is festive: the priest, the wedding guests, flower girls, bridesmaids and relatives of the bride and groom have all had enormous amounts of plastic surgery done in a vain attempt to resemble ants (the vanity which prompted them to this pre-wedding surgery was done to resemble tiny collapsible game hunters on safari which could be placed in one's wallet to tackle any feral cowhide ghosts roaming in the billfold tempting the statesmen on the bills to either milk or lasso them).

The church is empty except for a podium where the wedding cake sits looking like an anteater's brain. The bride and groom statues standing vertically on top of the cake personify the anteater's long narrow snout and tongue.

When the groom meets the bride, she tells him that an inverse wedding will take place where the wedding cake eats the guests, and the couple to be joined in union make the commitment never to see each other ever again, the marriage ritual being consummated when the couple promise to devote their lives to shouting apple pie recipes at vacuum cleaner attachments which were lost by the couple's parents over the years. The groom states that a vast genealogy composed of one's ancestors' galoshes in a world where it never has or never will rain, would more appropriately consummate a marriage.

He then has the bride stand at the podium with him where they cut themselves pieces of cake. The bride statue who is the anteater's snout sticks out the groom statue who is the tongue; they skillfully maneuver themselves, pulling pieces of cake off the couple's plates, reassembling their parts like a puzzle. The cake statues have the rare coordination of a protean being who can make anthill populations in Mozambique vanish while simultaneously encased in cellophane wrappers in the party accessory aisles of stationary stores in America. The cake cutting process repeats itself for a thousand years, during which time the groom was heard repeating something vague about those who are denied their own weddings should at least be entitled to the simple pleasure of eating one's own wedding cake. Why, he asks after a thousand futile attempts at indulging in one of the finest gustatory pleasures, does one feel he has spent the best years of his life performing an autopsy which prevents itself from being a complete autopsy?

The Groom wonders how he will avoid the embarrassing situation of telling people who really employed him as a would-be cake server; how does one explain that one's Boss and one's job are identical and opposites, radically different from each other.

On a more optimistic note, he is part of a universal plan and evolutionary cycle: logically if he spends his life attempting to cut the cake, the generation after that will in fact cut the cake, the next generation putting cake on party plates; and onward to even more advanced beings with intentions of eating the cake, but who die out before the first bite, due to the arrival of the age of calcified icing and frosting, ending abruptly when semi-space-age beings evolve who can eat the hardened cake and who in the act of doing so are rendered obsolete by beings who can digest the cake, who are in turn outmoded by advanced space-age beings with superior low metabolisms who gain weight from the cake while living in a space age world with vast solar systems with planets filled with labyrinthine diet book libraries. Interplanetary travel taking place on immense library cards, wars are declared over overdue library books borrowed by one solar system from another. The effectiveness of a solar system's military defense depending on how widely differing their metabolic range is compared with their enemy's (if a high metabolic solar system invades a low one, the invaders will gain so much weight they will be taken corpulent prisoners of war by their enemies who seize and assimilate all the diet books from their planet).

At any rate, not to go off on a pseudo-mataphysical tangent which could be successfully refuted by an organization of dollhouse plumbers with lockjaw, concerning the matters at hand, it must be noted that the bride wondered just how there could be a truly festive atmosphere when one's coquetry and refined manners rest solely upon the fact that you have spent your best years for romance dabbling in vivisection; surely even the most untutored mind could recognize that to dabble in vivisection is as credible as fourteen Aztecs from a futuristic Dutch soap opera shampooing a muskox at a Y.M.C.A. in downtown Chicago.

She is perplexed over the fact that if the bride and groom statues on the wedding cake represent a microcosm of her and her fiancee's lives, then is she the anteater's snout and the groom the tongue or vice versa?

This unanswered question causes lifelong controversy for the couple, as well as the wealth and fame of numerous psychics, astrologers and marriage counselors, some of whom tell them they are both snouts one week and both tongues the next. Others advise them that there is considerable good luck in being the snout on leap year, so there is a bitter war every four years over the possession of this role.

Long after the wedding, long after the couple finally threw down their forks and cake servers and left the church, long after the traumatic incident of the couple's car being adorned with seven million anteater's tongues which were actually the wedding guests reincarnated as the very ones who ate them—this concept by the way, is not an advisable pastime, particularly if you are dying on the great plains of Africa and expect to be next year's beauty queen for the Miss America Pageant.

(For further information read "The Exotic Scavengers Fight for a Position in American Mass Voyeurism" by Jacob Rudesheim, who brilliantly examines why small town consumers of amateur skin magazines can't appreciate pin-ups of the spotted hyena minus the spots, and why lavish centerfolds explicitly revealing the sensuality and intricate convoluted skin folds on the necks of Ethiopian vultures will always remain inaccessible to even the most sensitive members of the Young Men's Rifle Association.)

In time the couple were often heard complaining that during all the prosperous child bearing years, through the destruction of an enclave of vacuum cleaner salesmen who lived on a ferris wheel, by a decade long hailstorm of lace doilies, through the controversial era when legendary tyrants arose from the dead to tattoo cassowaries at beauty pageants, during the lively age known as "the flour and butter left out of recipe epoch" when home economics teachers were entombed and fossilized beneath infinite layers of tollhouse cookie dough. Through all the most eventful periods of history, the couple spent their lives making futile attempts at cutting themselves pieces of wedding cake which may not even be cake at all.

Long before any of this lamenting took place, when the couple left the church and arrived at their suburban home, the groom's lungs collapsed because the pink flamingos on the front lawn were more virile than himself. When the bride noticed this she decided to live on the front lawn and attempt to find out which flamingo made which lung collapse (she earns a degree in lungs collapsing due to husbands comparing their virility to lawn statuary).

The convalescing groom soon moved her inside the house because the flamingos layed eggs in her eye sockets which rolled inside her head, inexplicably causing the neighbors to mistake her for a bubble gum machine from the neck up.

Eventually a child is born to the couple who lives inside the bride's ribcage where he stretches his tail upward, holding it inside her head to incubate the flamingo eggs; when the eggs hatch the young flamingos eat away the tail because it exhibits the imposing manner of a nosy thermometer with a spine that is taking the temperature of the bride's thoughts about her controversial degree.

The child's tail continues growing back and the fledgling lawn statuary continue eating it off; this process repeats itself for a million years during which time many a passerby on the street could be heard to utter that hard times had truly come when the progeny of our lawn statuary spent their lives attempting to do what evolution already did better, although in years to come it became known that they made evolution obsolete. When announced publicly that an artificial fledgling flamingo was responsible for man walking erect, there was a world-wide echo of resonant apoplexy which occurred because of the sudden realization that a time will come when lawn statuary is no longer fashionable, and also because it would be a shame to have the advancing human mind come to a standstill because of the disappearance of kitsch.

THE OLFACTORY INVERSION

A man's sense of smell is reversed so fragrances smell like stenches and vice versa.

His nose has dyslexia.

To skip through a field of lilacs in early spring is equivalent to being tethered to a corpse during the high heat of summer.

The aroma of freshly baked bread is like the effluvia from an army's combat boots after marching through swamps for several weeks without stopping.

When the nose has dyslexia, the conventions of clean and dirty mutate amuck -

Nightmares of being dunked in vats of perfume become the norm -

Social status disintegrates and intimacy with a skunk brings joy -

The man burrows into remote dung heaps further and further away from the tyrannies of soap –

When the nose has dyslexia, predictable roles and behavior are scrambled anew -

Musk entrenched supermen get stampeded by berserk fawns in heat -

Germ-Phobics fondle dung beetles who, with freshly-molested vigor, do hind leg roll ups of squeeky clean solid citizens -

A prudish school marm finds a hidden rabid snapping turtle in her soul after being bitten by rotten apples given jaws by the teacher's pet gone astray -

When the nose has dyslexia, rampant desire surpasses grandiose expectation.

A wart on a baboon's ass blossoms into a more fragrant-than-thou perfume garden berry infecting a bestial psychopath who then penetrates with valor the furious posteriors of mandrills shimmying with profane delight -

Eager vines of algae growing up from centuries of neglected teeth, climb greedily towards the fortune of a fresh breath heiress -

Gooey-Pollyannas wash their mouths out with soap before reciting mantras of bland nicety to contrite career criminals gnawing on clean conscience bunions jutting from angel's feet -

When the nose has dyslexia, sacred values of societal dust are sculpted into new poisons by the playful rogue nostril metastasizing -

The Outhouse-Leper becomes a vengeful king, skinning the pillars of communities, turning the hides into outhouse doormats -

Blind Peeping Toms suddenly regain their sight munching on outhouse-doormat-brittle—thus seeing and tasting time honored models of proper conduct -

Yeast-Infected Vaginas curtsy with hypnotic finesse, flirting with clownish tumescent yam jam giraffes, spurting forth voyeurs turning into martyrs, turning into manic surgeons whittling skunky joy toys in a sleepless scalpel trance -

When the nose has dyslexia, the lightning of childhood memory strikes unlikely victims—oceans of crystallized feelings awaken from deep sleeps re-inventing the heart-

A hardened Loan Shark gets entangled, softened and diced up by the frail sadnesses evoked by the rubbery wet scent of his baby sister's favorite dolly lost in a distant rainstorm -

A loud-mouthed schoolyard bully becomes a mute wise old sage, transcending all utterance, ruminating inwardly, building shrines of cookie crumb folly from the remnants of desserts the bully once coerced from the trembling hands of weaklings entombed in the bowels of forgotten grammar school lunch rooms -

The cold stares of ultra strict baby sitters, soberly stretch a whiny little brat's dirty diapers into an almighty circus tent tundra sheltering cleaner than clean orphans sired by soap bubbles popping -

When the nose has dyslexia, embarrassment lurks in excess.

The man narrowly escapes the lewd clutches of Germ-Phobics hiding in lairs of undigested corn kernels waiting to leap out and fondle him.

He burrows inexorably deeper into remote dung heaps further and further away from the tyrannies of soap, eventually reaching paradise, where fragrant nirvana is sweetest, and stench lost its voice to the carrion bird who sings dirty in reverse.

The man enters The-Nose-Has-Dyslexia restaurant, ordering a Skunky-Joy-Toy-kiss smothered in freshly molested dung beetle sauce.

As frail, diced-up cubes of sensitive Loan Shark say grace, crowds of manic surgeons saddened by lost wet dollies, serve the meal in a sleepless scalpel trance -

The man tastes paradise, blessed by the voice of stench stolen by the carrion bird who sings dirty in reverse.

Suddenly The-Outhouse-Leper-Turned-Vengeful-King appears, interrupting the man eating, pedantically assailing him with correct table manner etiquette, forcing a squeeky clean knife and fork into his dungy hands , , ,

STATUS

A man lives inside the anus of a giant mythological pig with 14 karat gold bristles and onyx hooves.

His head is a tiny nodule peeking from between the pig's buttocks and capped by its curly tail coiling down upon the man's pate like a crown.

An etiquette book is fastened to the man's neck with a diamond-studded collar. The etiquette book is an albatross of rules for the proper maintenance of a regal back-door bestiality.

The anus has status, and the man is not a mere suppository.

The anus has been designed by an elite cadre of specialists who measured its diameter and depth to ensure that the man fit snugly along the anal canal with the bottoms of his feet pressing against the pig's large intestine.

The pig is mounted on a huge red carpeted platform which is carried on the shoulders of thousands of anonymous slaves sweating below. The gold bristles sparkle in the sun making the spectacle visible from great distances as it moves slowly through a pastoral landscape.

Crowds of social-climbing nomads follow the pig and scheme about rewriting the rules of the etiquette book, usurping the man by reducing him to a lowly suppository which the pig farts into oblivion, leaving its anus vacant for the occupancy of the nomads.

For idle amusement, the man plucks a gold bristle from the pig's tail with his teeth, spitting it down to crowds of nomads fighting over it mercilessly...

THE FOOL

A fool, fat sluggish and smug, was turned into a bowling ball by a gang of husky drooling village idiots.

With pontifical glee, the fool had waddled onto the idiots' grassy flatland turf, making the fateful mistake of underestimating their strength and ability.

The fool felt superior to the idiots, and feared not the clumsy thrusts of their silly toy swords slicing off his blubbery arms and his legs becoming an instant set of bowling pins.

The bowling ball had flawless symmetry, and was designed with a care, planning, and precision the fool knew the idiots to be incapable of.

The fool's overwrought brain became a coastal plain between dwindling shoulder dough, as the bloated no-neck-wart of a head was flattened against chest caved into gut—the pliable mass grew ever rounder amidst diligent idiot fingers kneading plentiful supercilious blubber with clinical detachment, erasing wrinkled valley cracks between buttocks stretched flat—

extraneous runty pee-prick vanishing with a swatted bug splat! which the fool's plaintive ears had been deliberately left to hear—the tired lardy organs and rubbery no-name bones were fished out and pulverized by the idiots' fierce callused feet, reducing them to a magical grey powder, evenly blended throughout the bowling ball, endowing it with good luck, balance, and poise, needed to roll straight and smooth, knocking down its former extremities.

With meticulous cosmetic perfection, the gang of village idiots erased all blemishes, bumps, birthmarks and scars, sanding the perfectly round bowling ball with pebbles until it was seamless, uniform and sleek, projecting a functional no nonsense aura, totally at odds with the fool's folly.

The bowling ball was given a singular identity—silly toy swords playfully doodling it all over with a secret code, guaranteeing that it would never be mistaken for other, almost identical fools turned into bowling balls by rival gangs of village idiots.

The Alpha Idiot, a wild but discreet giant with huge hands and thick long fingers, stuck his thumb up the fool's shadowy orifice, planting weathered, gritty middle and ring fingers in finicky nostrils—trinity of fingers plunging deep into trinity of holes—gripping tightly the hefty violated mass embittered with too many grievances to ever be redressed.

As the Alpha Idiot slowly lifted the fool, the subordinates set up the bowling pins a distance away, erecting live, twitching, arm and leg blubber stumps, by rooting pudgy fingers and toes in the ground so the pins stood vertical and secure in the grassy flatland winds.

The Alpha Idiot swung his arm back and forth, carefully aiming at the pins, pausing to hold the ball still and aloft, outstretched arm showing off its strength, as the subordinates circled around him, sitting worshipfully, drooling in unison, gazing up with wide eyed wonderment at the fool who deigned to address the entire gang of village idiots with a lofty plaintive condescending voice of damnation: YOUR FLIMSY WEAPONS SHALL BE CULPABLE EVIDENCE INDICTING ALL OF YOU! RETARDATE IMPRECATIONS COME UNDONE!

With the dour authority of a judge, the fool stuck his severe accusing tongue down at the idiots, a silent gesture that wasn't understood any better than the fool's weighty studied words, which made less sense than birdsong, wind, or the pattering of raindrops upon thick heads.

With overblown verbose nonsense ringing in their ears, the idiots babbled, grunted and cooed, blissfully mimicking the fool's accusing tongue—silly toy swords pointing back at it, boldly declaring their innocence.

The Alpha Idiot threw the bowling ball towards the distant pins—the fool spiraling up into the sky with a deep sigh of relief—landing with an impudent thud upon the grassy flatland turf—rolling away from the gang of village idiots cheering with excitement—watching the bowling ball pick up speed, quickly vanishing from sight—moving far faster than the fool's ex-legs could ever waddle him in his pre-bowling ball days.

The distance between the point where the Alpha Idiot threw the bowling ball, and the area where the pins of fat limbs were set up, grew wider and wider apart as the fool rolled—uniform grassy flatland stretching forever in all directions—the gang of idiots receding in the distance far behind the fool and the pins of fat limbs far ahead vanishing into remote horizons.

The fool rolled through myriad phases of folly—

Plotting the linear path ahead with infallible mildewed logic proving he's a zigzagging square when in fact he's round and rolling straight—

Bullying frail little flowers with overrated intellect—

Invoking a deity to fight with over whether or not lima beans are green—

Finding unconditional love with a pebble a nut a twig and a slug—

Passing on his genes with old maids who bore clay children—

Telepathically commanding his ex-fat fingers and toes to uproot themselves and dig for glittering rich honey-coated grubs—

The fool thus setting himself up to be deprived of a meal he earned by the force of his folly—

Ex-fat fingers and toes starving and insulting the fool by feeding glittering rich honey coated grubs to undeserving old maids and ungrateful clay children-

Ex-fat fingers and toes playing the fool like an ocarina—

Satiated old maids and clay children dancing to ocarina music in distant dreams of village idiots sleeping in a pile like a large litter of pampered puppies—

Ocarina music tootling across the grassy flatlands, attracting an ostrich-of- befuddlehood, bored with the platitudes of sand, who buried his head up the fool's behind, running for great distances with the bowling ball dangling from its long swivelling neck; poking around the moist angry rectum, reading the fires of profundity in the Alpha Idiot's thumbprint and hurling the fool off its neck with a sudden spasmodic jerk—

The fool flew high in the sky as spasms from the ostrich-of-befuddlehood's neck raced through him making him vibrate and change color as he slowly fell—

Turning black and blue with vital lessons of life never learned—fungus-fawn-fuchsia with shades of missing wisdom—enticing apple red with avoidance of truth—sad gold with false pride—mock humble transparent blue—shocking faux pas pink—mulish purple pomp—slothful salmon shuddering to be seen bumming downstream—greedy pigeon gray—erring fact orange—hiding from the enemy burnt sienna—slapped by the enemy raw sienna—bring the enemy to justice silver—murky lying water—muddy ochre logic—self righteous paisley peach—do-no-wrong grey area gone—subtle puddle ruffle puce—memory lead—virtue dead—rude officious lima bean green—lima bean green never to be seen refuted by fact—banana rot blue black brown spot yellow and proudly eggish antique white with a first memory of precocious pre-natal folly—

Mellifluous ocarina music, rich in subtle tones of soft gentle pity, poured out of the multihued fool as manic phantom ex-fat fingers and toes winged through the air, circling the falling bowling ball, plugging, unplugging and blowing wind into the trinity of holes.

Just before the fool fell to the ground, emaciated tearful pickpockets who robbed the fool in his pre-bowling ball days, suddenly appeared wearing thick layers of the fool's baggy tattered old clothing.

The pickpockets acted as pillows of redemption, cushioning the fool's fall and gently rolling him on his way—

The fool soon passed another fool, fat sluggish and smug, also turned into a bowling ball which rolled diagonally across his path destined to strike down another set of far off pins of human limbs.

The two fools were identical, differing only in invisible secret codes doodled on them by the silly toy swords of their makers.

The two fools didn't recognize each other and had an instant mutual revulsion, exchanging identical hateful grimaces as they rolled past each other.

The fool passed the Laughingstock-Reservoir, stopping to drink of the bile of whoever made a fool out of the fool and all whom the fool once fooled.

While quenching his thirst, he gazed at his reflection in the murky brown pool, seeing triumphant swarms of charlatans agog: snarling saints who kicked him, smirking con artists grown rich off revenues of suckerdom, the daft powers behind the throne of the ostrich-of-befuddlehood, redeemed, unredeemable pickpockets who depended on the fool cushioning his fall with plans of robbing him again, the fool's proud parents begetting new fool larva each time they smiled, a throbbing anguished pyramid of ten million identical bowling balls all sticking their tongues out at the fool, sultry pouting prostitutes with lonesome quivering breasts and poison nipples sucked for a hefty price, orphaned clay daughters sculpting themselves into mudpies of temptation flung at lusty shameless father fools, frail crazy old ladies and goofy blind children only the sickest coward would exploit, squirrels cheated of breadcrumbs thrown ball bearings instead, squirrels poisoned with acorns laced with lead, squirrel mummies gnawing the fool like a nut, squirrels reborn burying the fool in their gut.

The fool drank deeply of the bile which made him so fat, the fatness smothered all foolish excess.

The Laughingstock Reservoir turned into a giant wet murky bilious grin, laughing at the excess of fatness smothering the excess of foolishness.

The murky bilious wet laughter echoed far across the grassy flatlands, reverberating deep in the soul of the fool who was suddenly stricken with a clear balanced mind, filled with deep sadness, embarrassment and regret realizing for the first time who he was.

The fires of profundity in the Alpha Idiot's thumbprint shot from the fool's rectum inward, invading every cell of his sorrowful being, permeating the soul, burning up a vast accumulation of petty egotism, thumbprint flames ensnaring and transforming limitations and shortcomings, rapidly maturing him beyond all humanity, perfect and flawed, ridged, whorled thumbprint rings whittling him into the seed of every tree that ever existed. Thumbprint ring embers glowing with the missing link between dragon flies and hummingbirds, thumbprint smokerings spiralling upward cradling the great mother of all wings, sowing the seed of every tree across tranquil skies.

The primeval thunderclap of the bowling ball striking down the pins of human limbs rang out across the grassy flatlands, pounding the eardrums of the gang of village idiots brandishing their silly toy swords shining with victory.

The Alpha Idiot glowed with distinction, staring with blank humility at his left thumb, equal to birdsong, wind, or the pattering of raindrops upon thick heads.

The subordinate idiots drooled, babbled, grunted and cooed, sniffing the air, picking up the scent of a new fool approaching on the horizon about to wander onto their turf and make the fateful mistake of underestimating them.

THE WIDOW'S PEAK GHOST

A man traveling the route of his hairline finds the ghost of his widow's peak buried in a pore of scalp oil dust.

He unearths the remote area where his hairline began, charting the stages of receding which follow, making note of a dent mid-pate caused during a dispute when agents of anti-testosterone tried to dissuade the hairline from a life of receding.

On his backward climb he discovers his aging process in reverse, drifting down his pate on the way back from gleaming.

The man fastens the ghost of his widow's peak to his hairline for a hook; lowering it down a cranial pore like an eskimo fishing through a hole in the arctic ice.

He dips into his brain, angling for a memory of his youthful self looking in the mirror surveying the budding corners of his forehead starting to widen and gleam . . .

THE FUNERAL SERVICE

In a major medical school an anatomy teacher who is half tiger and half rubber ostrich, lives inside a cadaver on a dissecting table. He gives his lectures and directs his students by wrapping his long flexible striped neck through the bars of the cadaver's rib cage, making it look like a hand-woven basket. He rests his head on the palm of the left hand while directing the students' scalpel knives and scissors with the whiskers on his beak.

As time passes, the students remove the brain, stomach, intestines and heart, holding them aloft, offering them as Christmas tree ornaments for the teacher. The teacher graciously thanks his students, hanging the organs on the stripes on his neck. The brain, studded with leopard-spot-convolutions contrasts well with the neck stripes causing the teacher to believe that all interior decorators would approve of this. The teacher noticed a student staring with pious lust at his striped rubbery plumage as though it were angel wings on the cadaver's rib cage.

The teacher was quite offended, first contemplating placing a jar of embalming fluid on top of the student's head for a dunce cap. Instead the teacher's neck stripes expel him from the medical school permanently, dragging him out the front door, stripes coiling around the student's hands, neck and feet. When the stripes are finished they sterilize themselves with soap, quietly spiraling around the teacher's neck and dropping back onto his plumage.

The expelled medical student lies outside on the street, catatonic with his mouth wide open like a large mouth bass until two benevolent undertakers, a tattoo artist, and a pregnant mannequin, take him to their cemetery where all the dead sit astride their tombstones listening to popular music on radios while perusing yellowing women's domestic magazines from a bygone age, older than the bone dust of pharaohs.

The medical student keeps his mouth wide open, miming the round sculpted puffs of curly hair on a white toy poodle who has just had a haircut. His tongue, jutting from his mouth, is a pink tombstone. His red lips are roses circling the grave.

The pregnant mannequin and the dead cook up cheese omelets and sugary rice puddings, dropping the meals down his throat, functioning like a conveyor belt in a meat packing plant.

The tattoo artist and the mannequin marvel over the bright festive color of the medical student's tongue. The dead are all envious because their tombstones are dull gray and rough while the medical student's tongue tombstone is bright, shiny, wet, and alive.

The mannequin and the tattoo artist try to convince the medical student to become a graveyard, insisting that this profession would more than compensate for his failure in medical school. At first the medical student disagrees, but finally is convinced of the practicality of the idea, seeing it is a much less morbid fate than becoming a doctor.

At the next meal, the dead all wear life jackets the mannequin has made for them. The mannequin feeds the student by dropping bits of food down his throat in a rhythmic pattern. Between each piece of food, one of the dead jumps down the medical student's throat.

At intervals the tattoo artist writes the names of the dead on the medical student's tongue. The names wear off from saliva, disappearing into the tastebuds each time a new arrival descends down the throat. When all of the dead have arrived inside the medical student they split up into different groups and classes. They live in their own separate societies, well-nourished by the rich meals the mannequin drops down to them.

The very ambitious live in the brain where they thrive on the medical student's encyclopedic knowledge of the biological sciences. Some of the dead surpass the medical student, getting medical degrees by studying at the core of the cerebral membrane.

The very religious live just beneath the eyes, looking like ladybugs trapped under the dome of a water bubble. They stare out of the eyes and see God, who is really the mannequin tirelessly preparing their meals.

Once a religious prophet crawled up the tongue and out of the medical student's mouth. Standing on the tip of the tongue, he jumped into the left eye as though it were a pond. The prophet told his disciples that he had experienced his own death, but had been instantly born again in the pond of the left eye, nursing on the pupil as though it were a cow's black udder.

The mouse builders live in the heart, kidneys, stomach and intestines. They hang their mice from the bars of the rib cage like rodent chandeliers.

The bowling league's territory is from the pelvic bone to the tips of the toes. The bowlers roll their balls downward through the marrows in the leg bones. The balls which get past the joints in the knees roll into the toes making them swell and wiggle for long periods of time.

The bowlers keep score on the spinal column when they are not fighting with a store clerk who jumps from vertebrae to vertebrae of the spine as though he were a wood thrush hopping from stones in a brook.

The larval angels, who are beauty school majors, live in the arms because when the medical student sleeps, he flaps his arms up and down like the wings the larval angels are waiting to grow.

The mannequin takes food orders like a waitress for the whole community inside its grave. Conflicts rarely arise except when the medical student starts sneezing because he is allergic to the spaghetti being dropped down his throat for the mouse builders to hang their mice. The builders are worried that if they hang the mice by their tails they will bite the tops of their heads or try to hypnotize them with their eyes.

Outside the medical student's body the tattoo artist and pregnant mannequin live in the cemetery with the deserted gray tombstones.

One day a girl comes to the cemetery, wheeling her dead husband in a red wagon. The girl complains that that her husband died in a pouch hanging under a pelican's beak. She is mournful, saying with deep regret that her husband died in darkness with crowds of fish packed in like millions of debauched men in a dimly lit bar.

The tattoo artist and the girl discuss funeral and burial arrangements while the mannequin, who is now bulbously pregnant, has cracks in her plaster stomach. The medical student trembles doubtfully, saying he doesn't know how to deliver babies, as the tattoo artist writes the dead man's name on his tongue. The girl lifts her husband up with one arm placing red roses on him plucked from the medical student's lips.

The mannequin starts to have labor pains; a tiny red head appears through a crack in her plaster stomach. The girl, with her free arm pulls the infant from the mannequin as she drops her husband into the medical student's mouth.

The bright red baby mannequin is stiffer than the starched clothes its mother wore before she escaped from a department store window display. Little price tags dangle from its toes and its body is shaped like a skinned minks' red eyes and the owner of a clothing department store.

The tattoo artist tries to circumcise the child, but the child pushes him away angrily.

The girl, the medical student, the tattoo artist, and the mannequin whose stomach is split open like the aftermath of an earthquake, all say in unison how adorable the new child is. They are silent when the child kneels on the medical student's lips reading the price tags tied to its toes. This is the funeral service for the girl's husband.

THE MAN IN THE COUCH

A man lives inside a couch with a spring stuck through his body like a skewer.

Stuck from nape to back ball with the spiral wound tool. His arms and legs are stretched across the webbing beneath his back, supporting him in his skeletal bed cell.

The rows of coils running across the oblong couch frame are hooked through rows of holes at opposite ends behind his head and feet.

The springs flanking his ankles and ribs are shiny copper, free of paint from hours of scrubbing with fingers and toes on sleepless days and nights while going through the motions of washing.

Prostrate in his cramped compact living space, he is a fugitive trapped in hiding, feeling his dry tongue against his lower lip in the darkness.

The man feels a grinding in his belly when he moves, lifting his head up from the pillow of coils jutting from his nape, his face brushing against the burlap lining above him and beneath the outer cushions.

He listens to his breathing with eyes ajar, as memories of washing dishes in the diner where he once worked flash through his head.

The world outside the couch is a room in a city boarding house. The smell of dirty laundry and stale cigarette smoke permeates the room. Beneath the sill of a dim window, piles of yellowing newspapers are scattered across the floor, making his outer cell a tabloid heaven. From the ceiling a bare light bulb shines above the luminous slip cover on the couch below. An aged girlie calendar and several karate posters hang on the walls with menopausal strength. At one end of the room is a neatly made bed and a dresser covered with bottles of aftershave, shaving cream dispensers, mountains of dull, soapy disposable razors, crumpled government envelopes, and loose change.

The couch, a limbo in a haven of isolation, is wedged between the bed and a radiator. With his head at the warm end, and his feet at the bed end, the man listens to the distant gurgling of flushing toilets and running faucets in bathrooms adjacent to his room. From the hallway, the distinct jovial voices of his neighbors ring faintly but relentlessly in his ears, growing muffled and inaudible as the ancient radiator hisses through the arm of the couch.

Once gregarious, the man in the couch held great parties in his room, but now his neighbors are strangers and don't visit. The isolation of his room wasn't enough, so he withdrew further, in quest of a local extreme.

The owner of the couch, who wears bright Hawaiian polo shirts, lives in the building, visiting the room daily, bringing a fresh slip cover and bowls of oatmeal for the man on the spring.

When the man hears the owner enter the room, he stretches his arms above his head, unhooking the top coil of his spring from the inner couch frame.

He maneuvers his torso in a spiral direction, kicking and pushing against the frame with stiff arms and legs—heaving himself with all his might as though on a manual rotisserie—wiping sweat from his face on the burlap lining beneath the outer cushions each time he spins around.

He spirals off along the route of his inner coil—riding the alimentary roller coaster through his innards—wounded on the battlefield of crisscrossing springs—the burgeoning rows of coils spiraling out of his crotch—encroaching on his dormant stillborn phallic member in a half-assed act of castration. Staring out across the expanse of copper webbing, falling off the end coil in a usual state of unhealing, he emerges from the couch to eat.

He covers his face with a tabloid newspaper to shield his eyes from the light. Crawling across the floor, rising in a bent squat, gripping the arm of the couch, he pulls himself up to a stooped position, never standing erect, circling the couch with a bent gait, climbing over the hissing radiator, peering through a hole in his tabloid mask, watching the owner glowing brightly in his Hawaiian polo shirt, a beacon of hope, sitting on his bed holding his bowl of oatmeal.

The owner hands him the bowl, the man taking it hesitantly, poking at the clotted oatmeal with his fingers curiously as though it were some unknown foreign substance discovered for the first time. Slowly he eats, gazing up at the karate posters on the walls, the invincible muscular men reminding him to persevere on the couch spring to attain a better fate in the afterlife.

The owner of the couch would like to pull the spring out of the man's body, casting him out of the couch and into the world, thus destroying the delirium of his martyred glory on the spit. Then the owner could take the couch back to his own room, restoring it to its natural condition, reupholstering the interior with a new set of springs. The owner first lent the man the couch to more comfortably accommodate his frequent party guests.

The owner decided to let the man stay on the spring because he enjoys the submissive look on his face as he emerges from the couch to eat.

When the man finishes his oatmeal, he shields his eyes from the light of the colorful tabloid newsprint pictures merging with the flowing palm trees and svelte brown hula-skirted dancing girls adorning the Hawaiian polo shirt of the owner.

He goes back into the couch, spiraling onto his spring, recovering from sensory overload, returning to memories of washing dishes in the diner where he once worked, rehooking the neck end of his spring so he lies level with rows of adjacent coils.

The outer cushions above him contract, pressing against the inner frame as the owner puts a new slip cover on the couch.

CAVIAR

A fossil-speck of caviar ricochets back & forth between a man's pompadour and a woman's bouffant hairdo.

The fragile delicacy is incubated as it flies between the two hairdos.

The caviar hatches in mid-air, & the ghost of a hair stylist dinosaur emerges wet & dated in a land of pomade & hair spray.

It penetrates the woman's bouffant, getting lost in a maze of pink curlers where it hides, worried that the couple will question it about the care of modern hair styles.

While drifting down the pink plastic corridors of the future, it prays for the day evolution will make hair obsolete.

With the two halves of its roe-shell it makes a pair of radar dishes to detect the modern waves of the couple's thoughts about primping, barbering & trips to the beauty parlor...

LADY IN TRANSIT

Wearing a long
roomy black skirt,
antique white
princess seamed
silk blouse and
burgundy ballet
flats, She's
squeezed in a front
corner seat of a
crowded, late
afternoon bus.

Her classic
feminine clothes
contrasting with
torn ranch pant
trendmongers
poked with shiny
barracuda lures
and generously
inked with prolific
stray creatures,
designer brand
ephemera
streaking across
loud threads.

In perfect muted
tones, the lady in
transit feels she
rises above the
vulgarity
surrounding her.

Propriety aside,
her aura isn't
fragile. Her face,
determined,
calculating and self
conscious, is
reminiscent of a
once disgraced
president.

She has the severe
perfectionism of a
dog breeder,
causing boy
Chihuahuas to sire
offspring with
Great Dane girls,
in quest of a
medium sized dog.
She'd doom litter
after litter of
endless wrongly
sized puppies too
short or tall,

zigzagged limbed,
crooked spined,
none conforming
to her precise
elusive
measurements of
medium sized dog.

To reap their
fortunes, She'd
poison
industrialists with
the glue from the
spines of moldy
etiquette books.

The vices of the
Lady in Transit are
hidden from view,
She must be
exonerated for her
shortcomings
because her space
is suddenly
violated by a man
who sits next to
her, his wide open
legs brushing
against her skirt.
In a voice as

formal as her
outfit, she tells the
man six times to
close his legs
because he's
touching her. Her
anger rising each
time she repeats
herself, but the
man rudely
ignores her,
refusing to close
his legs.

Defusing the
situation, a
chivalrous Man of
Honor, sitting
opposite her, offers
her his seat, which
she graciously
takes, thanking
him.

The chivalrous
man of honor had
been discreetly
admiring her legs,
smoother than a

voyeurs' eyeball.
He'd give her an
impromptu kiss in
the red giant
sunshine of an
uninhabitable
planet, taking a
taste of the lady in
transit into the
afterlife, but
decorum tames
the moment and
he wishes her a
pleasant evening as
he exits the bus.

THE SLEEPWALKER

Across frozen puddles, a sleepwalker glides on one foot, fitted by prankish hands with an old rusty ice skate.

Nodding, bending, pirouetting in the cold wind in a fluid precise ballet-

Opaque eye slits blind to an inky tutu fungus of old newspapers encircling his waist; flaking into yellow dust with each thrust and turn-

Migratory birds flying to warm childhood memory rest on the stubbly promontory of his lower jaw-

Stratospheric tooth fairies play sky dominoes with long fallen baby teeth-

Oyster shucking insomniacs about to crack open the sleepwalker to drink his pearly nectar and go to sleep, get stuck reading the ruse of brittle tutu newsprint-

Trauma of old news increasing their insomnia a thousandfold-

Ruffians without thumbs opposable, unable to grasp him, freeze into thwarted bully icicles shattering in the random path of the nimble thrusting ice-skate-

Fragrant morning squirrels, mistaking the sleepwalker for an acorn, try to bury him in the permafrost but he breaks free-

Marzipan amazons in electric skates do figure eights—jolting him with 10,000 volts of flirty neon pink eye candy flings-

Stampeding buffalo, deep in the sleepwalkers' burnt sienna redwood tree beard stubble, inhibit smitten amazons from tempting him to shave, thus saving the buffalo from extinction-

Sycophants oozing flattery about skating finesse, fail to impress the sleepwalker,sycophants in their own hot air, melting into high affectation lemonade sold to pompous dignitaries in danger of turning humble-

Loan sharks eaten by polar bears dwelling in the carnivores' liver, try to telepathically poison the sleepwalker with vitamin D toxicity-

Porcupine quills from polaris shooting from the sleepwalkers' coccyx bone, skewering loan shark telepathists vertically in the arctic ice-

Slumming aristocrats, vacationing in the novelty of the sleepwalkers' spartan aura, chip lurid ancient newsprint souvenirs from his inky tutu fungus-

Shady fugitives on the lam, burn evidence used against them in sparks flying from the ice skate blade-

Across frozen puddles, rising into glaciers, the sleepwalker glides on one foot, impervious to malignant intent-

Ugly laughter of all who tried to scar him twisting into coddling nursemaid lullabies, warming his frostbitten ears, driving him crookedly over the north landscape-

Nimble rusty ice-skate glittering with an aurora borealis of prankish blue fingerprints-

Flaking trails of yellow tutu fungi dust blowing in the wind attracting intrepid wolves-

THE BATTERY SONG

We are a squadron of tiny pink mailmen with artillery hanging from our bellybuttons.

While charting our mind's route in song we deliver parcels of luminous afterbirth gilded like brass trophies.

Our containers stand huddled together, a pregnant clique forming a fortress of swollen bellies with all of us stationed at the watery cores shielded from the air traffic of adolescent gossip.

We sing in unison through transparent lips of makeshift souls—our thin chain of voices ten strong—reverberating throughout the labyrinth of uterine walls, bringing an echo of letters of arrival to the domain of young motherhood to be.

Our song can be heard faintly beneath the sky of gossip as we bring news of the coming seismic shifts in our core's drainage pipes.

In our battery of double shelled brain-kernels packed up tight in cranial-womb-tissue, we are a linked barricade with our artillery -cords to guide us so we can foresee the curettage approaching from the east—and the water never breaking in the child's bane out of womb-lock coming out of the west—

We drift, delivering parcels of luminous afterbirth gilded like brass trophies pausing along our mind's route to jot down diagrams in our log books of a distant menopause creeping at dawn.

WHITE FUZZ

A man places a litter of newborn mice upon his pate to cure his baldness.

Albinos they are, cradle fresh, all pink and bald with red face dots where the eyes will be.

They blend in with the man's pate like a flesh-tone toupee, nursing on scalp oil and thus sprouting white fuzz, curing his baldness vicariously.

The mice went from bald to hairy as they aged, while the man's balding process was reversed, going from hairy to bald as he got older.

The man feels confused about his symbols of youth, pondering the two opposing processes of hair growth and loss.

He feels even older than he did when he was bald, now that he's got white fuzz, the only eyes to ever see his pate are the sprinkling of albino red dots looming like color blind measles unable to tell the difference between hair and skin.